WITH THIS PROMISE

Windswept Bay, Book Seven

DEBRA CLOPTON

With This Promise

School teacher Lana Presley has sworn off cowboys. Which should work fine since she's relocated from Texas and is happily adjusting to her new life in Windswept Bay. After a bad breakup-that involved her using her cheating ex as target practice for hurling chocolate covered cherries at…she's happy to be single. And happy not to have her protective brothers and dad meddling in her business. Settling down on the coast permanently, miles away from Texas, is looking perfect.

Then the drop-dead gorgeous cowboy, Cam Sinclair, comes to her rescue…several times and sets all of her carefully made plans into chaos.

Rancher Cam Sinclair is just in town for a few days on business then heading home to his ranch in Texas. He's got finding the right woman and settling down on his mind. And from the moment he meets spitfire Lana Presley she has his attention. But she's made it clear that Texas and cowboys are not in her plans for the future. Can a road trip and Cam...and love change her mind?

Things are getting a bit complicated on the shores of Windswept Bay! Come join the fun in With This Promise book 7 of this captivating series. You've watched the four Sinclair sisters fall in love now it's time to watch the five Sinclair brothers find the women of their dreams.

CHAPTER ONE

Cam Sinclair pulled into the parking lot of his family's resort, now run by his sisters. He was running late…but it couldn't be helped. He turned the engine off and as he started to get out of the truck, he spotted his brother Max jogging across the parking lot. Cam hopped from his own truck. "Hey, Max, what's your hurry?"

His younger brother saw him and altered his course toward him. "Cam, you made it. Slick move to be late for the auction."

Cam shrugged. "I couldn't help it. What are you

doing—dodging a date?"

"Nah, I got called out. The auction was almost over but I need to report for duty immediately. If you hurry, maybe you can take my place."

"I think I'm fine." He knew Max couldn't say a word about where he was going and might not even know at this moment where he was heading off to. He was proud of Max and worried for him at the same time, but Max loved what he did.

"Look, I hate to run, but I need to get there. As usual, I'll let all of you know when I'm back stateside." They hugged.

"You watch yourself, little brother."Cam didn't bother to tell him to be safe. That wasn't always a possibility, he had a feeling, with the top secret missions Max was involved in.

"I always do. Tell Levi to watch out for my pig while I'm gone." He grinned.

Cam watched him jog a few steps. "You and your pig. That's just not right. You need a wife to come home to, not a guard pig."

Max grinned. "Not the right time. But you, on the

other hand, are all set up for a wife, with your ranch in Texas and your advancing age."Max—being the youngest Sinclair brother at twenty-nine and Cam being the eldest at thirty-three—liked to rub in the four-year age difference.

"Who knows. Maybe I'll be married by the time you get home."

"Then you better hurry. This is supposed to be a short mission. In and out. Gotta go. I'll meet the new missus when I get back." He laughed over his shoulder and jogged off. Then he stopped and turned back. "Hey, Cam," he called, serious now. "Really, take care of yourself. Glad I got to see you before I left."

And then he jogged the rest of the way to his truck and was gone.

Cam watched him leave and fought to ignore the unease that churned in his stomach. *Max would be back.* Turning, he moved back to his truck and climbed back in to grab his keys and lock the doors. His brother had great instincts, a plus in his line of work, and in the short moments they'd talked Max had hit the target that had been nagging at Cam for the last few months.

He was ready to settle down.

But the last time he'd checked, it took the right woman to settle down with to make the equation work out right. As of yet, he hadn't found her. *The right woman.*

But he was open to meeting her any time she decided to show up. Though he doubted it would be before Max got home.

Lana Presley left the Valentine Bachelor Auction at the Windswept Bay Resort dateless, but smiling. She hadn't gone to find a date. She'd gone to see whether her friend, Jessica, would get one. And thankfully she had. Love was a wondrous thing…not that she was looking for it. But she still enjoyed the romance of it all when it worked out.

It was the crashing and burning that went along the way to finding love that she herself was weary of.

Still, the Sinclair sisters should be excited for themselves because their bachelor auction had been a huge hit. Especially for her friend Jessica and Levi

Sinclair. Her friend had been worrying her lately. Lana knew that Levi was good for her, so Lana had been rooting for the two to get together.

The fact that Jessica had come out of her shell and taken a chance on loving again was wonderful. Lana didn't know what went on after they left the auction together but she was excited to hear all about it. And she hoped they were now officially an item.

Lana had to admit that the auction had been an eye-opener. All the guys had been really having a great time and the Sinclair brothers had been so good-natured about the whole thing that just watching them had been entertaining. But one brother had been missing—the one she was curious about, Cameron—or Cam as they called him. He lived in Texas and owned a ranch. He was a cowboy rather than a beach boy. Not that any of the Sinclair men looked like boys but they had all settled in their hometown on the shores of gorgeous Windswept Bay.

Lana had heard some of the teachers talking about the brothers in the teacher's lounge at school. And she'd heard his name come up a few times. *And* because she was from Texas herself and she and her five brothers had been raised on a ranch, she had been curious about the brother who'd moved to Texas to become a rancher. Not that she was interested in any way, just curious about him. She'd had one too many dead-end relationships with cowboys to be thinking anything other than just plain curiosity about the man.

She'd actually moved to Windswept Bay to get away from cowboys—including her brothers and her dad. She needed space. She had begun to build her own life here and she really liked it. Though she did miss riding her horses. She had heard there was a small stable in town on the island; she planned to check it out tomorrow and was excited about the prospect of riding again.

She'd parked her truck at the back of the parking lot and finally reached it. Climbing inside the cab, she inserted the key and turned it. Instead of the engine firing up, all she heard was a dull clicking noise of a dead battery.

"No, come on." She groaned and tried again—as if that would change the fact that she had a dead battery.

She'd known her battery needed replacing and she hadn't stopped and changed it out. She was giving herself a good scolding when she noticed the truck lights go out not too far away from her. Only then did she realize that the truck parked across several parking spaces was pulling a horse trailer.

In between scolding herself, she wondered who was driving the rig. If there was one thing this Texas girl knew, it was to take care of her business. She should have stopped by the auto-parts store and picked up a battery right after this had happened the first time. Certainly the second time she'd had to get a jump from someone. But she hadn't and now she was serving the consequences, as her dad would say.

She shot a glance over at the truck but the parking lot lighting made it hard to make out who was driving.

The big rig made her think of her brothers and her dad—ranching and hauling horses or cattle was part of the job. Taking care of your business and equipment was also part of the job. They'd be giving her the dickens right now for letting this happen and stranding herself.

She leaned forward, popped the hood release and then exited the cab. She glanced over at the truck once more, curious who was driving it and staying at the resort. She strode to the front of the truck—which had also been used for hauling animals. She reached for the release lever and then pushed the hood up. She pulled out her phone, found the flashlight button and then grabbed the grill with one hand and placed her boot on the front fender. She was too short to do anything standing on the ground. She pulled herself up, leaned under the hood to peer into the dark cavity as she aimed her light on the engine.

"Do you need some light?"

*"What?"*Lana yelped, jumped and slammed her head into the hood before she lost her balance and slipped from the bumper. She would have fallen if strong arms hadn't caught her.

"Are you okay?" the man asked, holding her securely against his hard chest.

"Am I okay," she muttered, rubbed her head and glared at the man."Don't you know to warn a gal? You don't just walk up and scare a person." She struggled to get out of his arms. Her head throbbed, she probably had a goose egg the size of Texas on her forehead thanks to him.

"You're sure," he asked, sounding skeptical but setting her on her feet.

"Positive," she grunted and immediately backed away from him while still massaging her throbbing forehead.

"I apologize," he drawled, sounding truly concerned.

His tone wasn't completely Texan but sounded totally cowboy. She inhaled and tried to calm down as she focused on him. He tugged his hat off and it gave her a better view of his shadowed face. Whoa...she sucked in a breath. The resemblance to all the other Sinclair brothers was unmistakable so she knew instantly who she was looking at.

Cam Sinclair.

Oh, my...her thoughts stalled, her gaze caught by penetrating eyes glinting in the low light.

"Are you okay? I was trying to help. Not injure you."

He was tall, with striking features—even in the shadowy lights she could more than tell the man could cause traffic jams and break hearts too. Which she knew more than enough about.

She got a grip on her imagination. "I'm fine. And I'm sorry I got so upset. But just so you know, next time you come up on a woman in the darkness, give her little warning." She scowled, completely unsure why she was so irritated.

He flicked on his phone light and held out his hand."Let's start over. I'm Cam Sinclair. And I'd like to take a look under your hood if you'll let me."

Lana lost her voice.

"Are you okay?" he asked again. "You look pale in the light."

"Um, yes, I'm fine. Sorry."*What was wrong with her?* She'd seen plenty of good-looking cowboys in her day.

"So can I?"

"Can you what?"

"Look at the truck?"

She blinked and gave herself an imaginary kick in

the jeans. "Yes, sure."

"Are you sure you're feeling all right? You really do look a bit strained."

She nodded, feeling quite silly actually.

He moved to the truck and leaned under the hood, shining his light into the engine compartment."This is a mighty big truck for a small woman."

She stood on her tiptoes. Yes, she had big tires that hiked the truck up higher than a regular truck. "It's no bigger than yours over there."

He lifted his head to look at her. "Do you haul with this truck?"

"Not these days. But yes, I have."

He nodded, his expression thoughtful as he took that info in. She didn't elaborate. Although she knew who he was, she didn't feel the need to tell more.

He focused on the truck, jiggled a few things, took the cap off the radiator and replaced it. Checked the oil and then studied the battery. "I'm thinking it's the battery, so let's give it a try."

"That would be great. It's done this before."

"You'll need to get a new one tomorrow." He

cocked his head to the side and met her gaze with serious eyes that she couldn't make out the color of in the dim light. "Okay. Getting stranded isn't a good thing. Your husband or boyfriend can fix you up."

"Yes. Sure. Thank you." Her pulse bucked like a rodeo bull and it was irritating as fire. "And, it's all on me. I'm single and free and I'm the one who didn't get the battery." *Now why had she let that out? Too much information.*

Reminder to self: Cowboys are off my list of allowable attractions and I'd do well to remember that.

He didn't say anything, just tipped his head and strode off.

Lana watched every step he took.

Yup. The man looked fine in his jeans and boots. *Shoot. This would not do. Not at all.*

Cam moved his truck forward. The lady was irritated and had him wanting to smile. She definitely had a mind of her own. He hadn't meant to scare her but she'd grabbed his attention the minute she jumped from the seat of the truck. He'd watched her march to the front of her vehicle and push the hood open as if she knew what she was doing. When she'd hoisted her small self up onto the front bumper, he'd started moving as fast as he could toward her. He'd been so intent on offering her help, he hadn't thought about scaring her. He felt really bad about that—but when she'd fallen into his arms…he'd been glad he'd been there.

She was a spitfire, it was easy enough to see, and he recognized a Texas twang when he heard one. This was no Floridian. He pulled his truck up close enough to hers so the jumper cables would reach. Then he hopped out and got them out of the steel gear box mounted in the truck bed.

"I'm sorry, I didn't mean to be rude," she said when he walked back to her. "I'm Lana Presley. It's nice to meet you. I'm acquaintances with your sisters."

"Acquaintances?"He studied her.

"I'm fairly new in town and have just met them briefly."

"I see. Well, welcome to Windswept Bay. I can tell by your accent that you're a Texan. Are you any kin to Marcus Presley of the Presley Ranch?"In the darkness, it was hard to read her expression but he was pretty sure she stiffened.

"I might be. Is there a problem?"

The coolness in her tone startled him. He shrugged, curious about her now more than ever."No, ma'am, no problem." He applied the cables to each truck. "You can go crank it now."*The lady clearly didn't want to talk about any relation to the Presleys of Texas.*

She headed away and in a moment, the engine started. He removed the cables from the battery. His work was done. But he wasn't ready to say good-bye.

"Thanks."She came back to the front of the truck.

He pulled the hood down and closed it. "You're welcome. I'm glad I could help."

She pushed her wavy, dark hair behind her ear. She was pretty in a simple, no-nonsense kind of way. She had a wide mouth, almost too wide for her small face, and a square jaw that lifted in defiance, he'd learned, when she was tense. It had lifted when he'd asked about the Presley relationship. Now it lifted again and he found himself wanting to smile. He had a feeling that despite her size or her calm beauty that if she was riled up, she'd have a temper.

"I didn't mean to sound rude before. I just don't really know you."

He tipped his hat. "I understand. A lady can't be too careful. You need to get this battery fixed tomorrow."

She cleared her throat; he thought she was going to say more but instead she nodded and turned to go.

"Maybe I'll see you around while I'm here in town." He wasn't shy and she interested him.

She paused at the open door of the truck. "Maybe. But probably not. I was just here tonight for the bachelor auction."

"Ah, I see. Did you get one?"

In the shadowed light, he thought she cringed. "No. I didn't come for one."

And with that, she got in her truck and with a slight wave, she backed the truck out of the parking space and drove away.

Cam watched as Lana Presley pulled out of the parking lot. She had not been exactly rude and not exactly happy to be around him either. All he had done was help her. Despite his interest, there was no denying that she'd been a little prickly—and clearly not interested in anything he had to offer.

So why was he still mulling over thoughts of her as he entered the front entrance of the resort in search of someone from his family?

He wasn't sure whether the Valentine auction was over or whether anybody would still be around but just in case, he headed into the resort. Hauling horses from Texas to here was a long haul and he hadn't made it in time to help his sisters out. He hated to say it but he wasn't sorry he'd missed being in the auction. He was here on business, though they didn't know it, and he really didn't have time, even for a charity, to go on a date. He also wasn't real keen on the idea of being *bought* as a date.

He spotted his sister Cali entering from the back courtyard entrance of the resort.

He was the oldest son and she was the oldest daughter, so the two of them had always been close.

Her expression brightened the moment she saw him."Cam, you made it late but you made it! It's so great to see you."

"Hey, sis. Good to see you too."He hugged her and saw her husband Grant coming through the sliding doors."Grant, I see she didn't auction you off." He laughed and he shook hands with his friend.

"No." Grant grinned as Cali wrapped her arm around his waist and smiled up at him."She didn't auction me off, but they got everyone else auctioned off. It was a night to remember."

Cali smiled. "Jillian had a great idea. I just hope none of the dates turn into disasters."

"That wouldn't be good." Cam grimaced.

"No, it wouldn't. But the best part of the night was that Levi got bought by Jessica. Remember the lady he brought to Mom's birthday party?"

"Yeah, he brought her and her little boy, I remember. So she bought him?"

Cali smiled. "She did. It was awesome and

romantic. And made the whole evening worthwhile. Which was Jillian's ulterior motive in the whole episode."

"Well, that's great. Levi's starting to get to that age where he's looking to settle down."

Cali's expression brightened even brighter "So are you at that age?"

He was older than Levi and his twin Trent. "Yes, nosy sister, you heard correct. I am really starting to think about my future. And all my sisters getting married and being so happy has influenced me."

She laughed. "Yay."

Grant tugged her close. "Good to know. If you ask me, it's the smartest thing I ever did."

Cam looked to his good friend, who still owned a ranch next-door to his in Texas. "We both know it's the best thing that happened to you. You've never looked happier."

"You're right about that."

"You should have made it to the auction and gotten this ball rolling." Cali's eyes twinkled.

He laughed. "I think I can find my own way."

"Okay, good luck. So weren't you making a horse delivery or something?"

"I had some business I'm hoping to finalize tomorrow." He glanced at his watch. "I hate to run but I've got a trailer full of horses I need to tend to. I'll be around."

"Where are you boarding the horses? Are you staying at Mom and Dad's? You're more than welcome to stay with us."

He decided there was no reason not to tell. "I'm taking them out to Bess's horse stable down on the beach road."

"Of course, I should have known that but I heard she sold it suddenly. And that last week she left town and went to live with her sister."

Grant eyed him suspiciously. "Did you buy that place?"

Cam laughed, unable to keep his secret any longer. "I did."

"Oh my goodness," Cali exclaimed. "I can't believe it. Are you moving here?"

"You are full of questions. When I was here for

Shar's wedding, I dropped by to check on Bess. I hadn't seen her in a while and just thought I'd say hi. She taught me a lot about horses growing up and helped fulfill my dream of becoming a cowboy. While I was there, she asked me if I'd ever consider buying her place. She was ready to retire and so we struck a deal."

"I think that's wonderful. Mom is not going to believe this. Why didn't you tell her? Or us?"

"Because I wasn't certain Bess wasn't going to pull out of the deal. It's a sentimental sale. I only wanted her to be happy, so if she had decided at the last minute to keep the stables I didn't see any reason to get Mom and Dad's hopes up."

"I understand. Well, this is so exciting."

"I think it's great," Grant added. "I'll have to come out and ride some."

"I'll be going over it this week. Come out when you have time. I just stopped in to check on how the auction went, but I think I'm going to head over there now. It's been a long day."

And he was ready to see his place. When Bess had

asked him whether he'd be interested in the place, it had surprised him. But then, he'd looked around and been startled by the possibilities that he began to see. And the legacy that he had from Bess's patient lessons had meant the world to him. He didn't want to take the chance of some corporation coming in and buying this prime piece of property and doing away with the horses. That had been Bess's only stipulation: it would remain a stable. And that had suited him just fine.

Now he just had to decide how he was going to manage it from Texas.

CHAPTER TWO

It was a gorgeous morning and Lana woke at sunrise, excited about the idea of going to the stables and riding. It had been awhile since she'd ridden and now she was suddenly eager and couldn't get there fast enough.

She was, after all, a cowgirl at heart and she had not left the love of the lifestyle behind; she'd just needed a break from it. And riding horses on the beach sounded like heaven.

She was surprised and pleased when her truck cranked. She had let it charge for a while last night before she finally turned off the engine and gone in to go to bed. That boost obviously worked.

She was normally more responsible about her business but the truck was fine this morning, so she'd stop by after riding and get a new battery. The idea of the early morning ride—on a beach, even—was just too appealing.

The stables were easy to find, just off the main road past the resort. There was a small sign beside the turn that led down to the property. Everything looked really quiet as she pulled through the small entrance of Bess's Horse Stables. The barns were off to the left and the house was on the right. It was a small ranch style home that looked out of place here in Florida and so near the beach. It made her think that the owner must have been from Texas.

Parking her truck, she got out and surveyed the area. She spotted a horse trailer peeking out from behind the stables. A familiar truck also stuck out of a barn across the way. She headed toward the truck, wondering where everyone was. *Tourists must not like to ride early.*

Life on the ranch always started early and riding was the best in the early mornings when the sun was not too hot. She heard the soft nicker of horses as she entered the double doors of the stable. Sunlight filtered in from the open doors and Lana paused to breathe in the scent of fresh hay and feed. The stables were clean; the scent told the tale. Ten horses looked over the stalls at her.

She smiled in response. Something in her heart clicked over with emotion. *Why had she waited this long before coming here to ride?*

"Hey there, pretty girl." She could hear the excitement in her own voice as she talked softly to the mare in the first stall. She went from stall to stall, getting welcoming nudges from the horses.

These horses were used to having people around.

She was scratching the forehead of the pretty chestnut mare when the crunch of boots alerted her to someone approaching. She turned just in time to see a cowboy carrying a bale of hay enter from the opposite end of the building.

He stopped. It was Cam Sinclair.

"Um, hello," she said, stunned to see him again. Though the truck had looked familiar, black diesel Dodges were not uncommon. "I'm startled to see you again."*Way to say something coherent.*

The truth was, the cowboy was drop-dead handsome in daylight. The dim parking lot lighting had not done him justice.

You are not interested in cowboys.

The voice in her head snapped at her. No, she wasn't. She'd given them up after last year's deception by her ex-boyfriend.

She halted her runaway thoughts. In the span of about two seconds, her thoughts had really gotten out of line.

He looked startled himself. "Good morning."He came her way. "The stables are closed. Sorry, do you ride here?"

Disappointment filled her. "No. Bummer. This is my first attempt to come out for a ride. I haven't ridden since I moved to Florida. And for some reason, yesterday I just got thinking about it and decided that today would be a good day to start again. Once I started thinking about it, I couldn't wait to get here. I was really looking forward to taking my first ride on the beach. Is the lady who owns the place ill?"

He opened a stall and went inside. Out of habit from years growing up feeding stock, she moved to the gate and automatically closed it behind him. She waited as he put a portion of the hay into the horse's trough and when he came back her way, she opened the stall gate for him and let him through.

He grinned. "It's obvious you know your way around the stable."

She laughed. "Old habits die hard. I've put a lot of hay in a lot of stalls in my day."

He walked to the next stall and she walked beside him and opened the gate for him.

"Thanks. Bess retired." He put the hay in the trough and came back toward her. "I just bought the place. This is my first day. You must've missed the sign that said Closed."

"I guess I did. You bought the place?" she asked, when clearly he'd just said so. "I mean, sorry, that's none of my business. I'd just heard you had a ranch in

Texas."

"I do; that's where I live. But this place has sentimental value to me. Bess and I didn't want a corporation to buy it. She asked me to consider it since she was ready to retire. She and her sister wanted to start traveling. I wanted to preserve the place too, so now I'm the owner of a stable on the beach and a ranch in Texas."

She smiled at the way he said it. "Then you are going to have your hands full."

"Very." He entered the next stall and they went through the routine until all the bales of hay ran out. "Life is an adventure."

"True. Oh, this mare is expecting!"

"Yeah, any day."

"I love foals. Love watching them right after they're born as they get their feet under them. It's so sweet. I've helped deliver a lot of them. If you need any help, let me know."

"Thanks. So, are you related to Marcus Presley?" He squinted at her. "None of my business but you have my curiosity up."

"I'd just met you. But, yes, he's my dad."

"No wonder you've been raised up on a ranch. He's got a big spread."

"Yes, he does. Look, you've got things to do. I should go. This is exciting that you bought this place. I'll leave and let you get back to what you are doing and maybe later, after you reopen, I'll come out and get my ride on the beach."

She backed toward the exit, oddly reluctant to go. Cam Sinclair was successful, good-looking, tall, dark, and handsome, and had a very sexy smile. And he was single. She *should* be reluctant to leave. She was female, had blood pumping through her body, and she was single herself. She would be crazy not to be reluctant to leave. Except she'd too recently had her heart broken by one devastatingly-handsome heartbreaker of a cowboy and decided no more.

And that was what she needed to keep in mind.

Cam watched her backing away. "Hey, I'm about to saddle up and ride the property. If you'd like, you can come along."

She should leave but she really wanted to ride. "I

guess that would be great—if you're sure." She inwardly cringed. She knew she should get her rump in gear and get off the property now.

He flashed a smile and her heart did an extra giddy-up. *Dad-gum-it.*

He removed his hat, exposing a dark, thick head of hair. "I'm sure."

"Then, okay, thanks. Which one do I saddle up?"

Cam glanced over at Lana riding next to him on the chestnut mare. She was a good rider. It was easy to tell she'd grown up in a saddle. He didn't know a lot about the Presleys other than they owned a big ranch in central Texas and raised prize-winning horses and cattle. And there was some controversy that went along with them a few years back. He even thought one of the brothers might have gone to jail at some point. Which, come to think of it, was probably the real reason she had been a little prickly last night when he asked whether she was related to the Presleys from Texas.

"So what do you think?" He glanced around at the

shoreline as they rode the horses out onto the sand. It was beautiful and had been a long time since he had ridden on a beach. He had missed it. There was a difference in riding in the pastures in Texas, which he loved, and riding on a tropical beach, which was relaxing and satisfying in a different way.

"It's beautiful."

Her voice, filled with awe, drew his gaze. Her emerald eyes sparkled in the sunlight. She pushed a strand of dark hair behind her ear as she studied the horizon and the topaz water rolling in.

"This is the life."

"Yeah, it is. I had forgotten what it was like riding on the beach."

"So why did you leave the beach?" she asked. "From what I've heard—yes, I've heard a few rumors about you," she said when he shot her a skeptical look. "I've heard that you basically left here and bought a ranch in Texas when you were young."

"I was twenty-two. Almost eleven years ago. I found the property and negotiated for it and got a great buy in a bad market. I bought as much land around it over the years as I could get my hands on, adding to it here and there until I now have a nice-sized place scattered over three counties. I'm proud of my ranch."

"Why Texas? There's a lot of ranches in Florida. Why not buy one here?"

The gentle rocking motion of the horse as it walked through the thick white sand had a way of slowing time, he thought as he let his mind wander back to that moment when he knew it was time to head that way. "I don't know. I was born loving Westerns on TV and I guess Texas just called to me. I wanted to be there all my life. It was just a few thousand miles away."

She laughed. "True. Did you try to get your parents to move there?"

"Yes, I did. But since that wasn't a possibility, they got me horse riding lessons."

"Sweet. My brothers love Texas and I don't think you could pry them out of there. Of course, they were born there. But it's in their blood."

He shot her a glance. "So why are you here? Texas girl on an island off the coast of Florida, having to hunt out a horse at a stable to get some riding in?"

She hesitated. "There are a lot of reasons. Job. I wanted to see new sights. I love beaches."

"But there's more," he said.

"You're very perceptive," she said, in a husky Texas twang.

"No, just a gut feeling there's more."

"Family—as in big brothers and dad interference. I love them dearly but a girl can only take so much meddling in all aspects of her life." She made a cute face.

She was funny. "I've known you a couple hours and I can tell you can handle yourself. You would have told your brothers to go jump off a roof. And your dad, you would've told him too, in a kind way, to back off. Nope, for you to leave your family, state, and horses behind, there's more."

She stared at him. "You think you know everything,"

He grinned. "So what was it? Bad breakup?"

"Yes. As a matter of fact. I was the jilted girlfriend and I got tired of seeing my ex and my best friend strutting around town and everywhere else I went. Small towns are notorious for that."

"So it hurt you a lot to see them together? I'm sure that was rough. But if they were those kind of people, you're better off without either one of them."

"It was irritating. If there's one thing I don't like, it's being strung along. And I have a temper and I hold grudges, maybe that's a Texas thing, but I have never appreciated being used. Nor do I appreciate being really, really mad. And when I walked down the streets of my hometown, every time I saw my ex and my best friend all smoochy, smoochy, it was galling. And it put me being the talk of the town. I got so mad. I didn't think that was very becoming for a first grade teacher." She took a deep breath and then started again. "It was the tempting urge to go up to them and trip them or say something snarky to them and feeling like that all the time really got to me. It was always there. Behaving badly was not something I wanted to do…not over him and I was in danger of doing just that. And that would only have embarrassed me in front of the whole town, so I left. I took myself out of the equation."

Again, he laughed in disbelief. "You let them run you out of town?"

She frowned. "My brothers and my daddy did not understand it either and said the same thing. And they made their opinion known loud and clear. No, I left because I wanted to do my own thing and here I am riding horses on the beautiful beach with the breeze blowing through my hair, a handsome cowboy at my side. What is there not to like here? Oh, and no ex-boyfriend and my lousy ex-girlfriend rubbing my ignorance in my face."

Cam's saddle creaked as he turned to look directly at her. He wasn't exactly sure what to think about Lana Presley except that he liked her. "I like your honesty." And he had a feeling that her ex would one day regret what he had done.

"Oh, and don't let the good-looking cowboy part go to your head," she warned, eyes twinkling. "I was just talking."

"Hurting my ego, that's what you're doing. For a moment there, I hoped you thought I was cute," he teased. "I think that ex-boyfriend of yours is going to really regret what he did one day. It's his loss and I mean it."

She studied him and then clicked her heels gently to set the horse moving forward. Cam did the same. "Thank you," she said. "I'm over him. But I'm not over the fact that I wasted a couple years of my life on that piece of junk. Now I'm finding my own way. And I have no plans to risk my heart right now. That was several months of turmoil. I do not want a repeat for a very long time."

"I find it interesting that you think you'll do that again. I have a feeling that's a mistake you will never make again. When you start dating, you'll know the integrity of the guy you're about to date. You won't risk giving a guy the time of day who isn't worth your time."

"Ah, so easily said, but knowing who is and who isn't is tricky. And the hard part."She slid him a glance and nodded. "But still, you got that right on the money, no matter how hard it is."

Cam could not help himself and grinned. "I have to tell you, this has been one interesting ride. You're welcome to come out here and ride anytime you want to."

She winked at him. "Why, thank you, sir. I just might. But this is the last time I'm going to mention my past. I came out here to ride, to get my head on straight. Not to relive my sordid history."

"I won't be prying, so no worries about that."

"So how about you? You're what, thirty-two or thirty-three? Single and you seem to have recognized my bad relationship history like a man who knows something about it from up close and personal. What gives?"

"Not what you think. I've had my share of horrible relationships but I haven't had a serious relationship. You forget, I have four sisters. And four brothers. I've lived through this numerous times."

"Oh, right. I'm sure you did." She smiled, wincing. "Four sisters."

He smiled. She was the tell-it-like-it-was kind of woman. And he had a feeling that when she did fall in love that the poor sucker was going to have his hands full.

CHAPTER THREE

Lana could not believe she'd told Cam about her ridiculous, pathetic love life. She hadn't even told Jessica that she had come here partly because of a failed relationship. It was embarrassing and for some odd and crazy reason, she had just told him— practically a stranger—her business.

It was time to change the subject. "This place is really lovely. I mean it. I can totally understand why you bought it."

He stared toward the trees and the paths that she could see weaving through them in this tropical setting.

It was not your common Texas landscape, with oak trees and mesquite but instead, it was colorful flowering trees and palms and there was the ever-growing groundcover beach morning glory with its lavender flowers still open.

"We'll need to turn and head up through there and follow the boundary line. I'll lead; it's a single file path. This place meant a lot to me when I was a kid." He pulled on the reins so that his horse slowed. She did the same just as a wave hit a rock in the water beside her and the sea spray suddenly splashed over them.

She laughed. "Now that is different from riding horses in Texas."

Cam laughed too. "Do you need a towel?"

Pushing her damp hair from her face, she laughed again. "No, it's great. I love it. Thank you for letting me come along."

He got a speculative look on his face. "Come on," he said, and then before she knew what he was doing, he had his horse loping along the beach.

"Yes!"Lana exclaimed and set her horse loping after him. He glanced over his shoulder; his expression radiated happiness and she felt exactly that—the salt air, the warmth of the rising sun, and the feel of the horse loping over the firm, wet sand. And a fine-looking cowboy smiling at her as he challenged her to catch him.

She urged the mare into a gallop and leaned forward as she caught him. "This is awesome."

"I thought you'd like it."

"Yes, I do." He rode beside her along the pristine coastline and then they slowed back to a lope and then a walk. Both were smiling from the joy of the ride.

"That was amazing."

"Agreed. I had forgotten how fun riding on the beach is."

"And you didn't have a cow to rope." She chuckled, enjoying his reactions.

More than she wanted to.

Moments later, they entered the trees to check out the interior of the property.

"You said you got lessons from Bess early on.

How did that happen? Did you drive your parents crazy trying to get them to move to Texas?"

"I did. I was only five. Finally, my mom learned of the stables and signed me up for lessons for my sixth birthday. I took to it like a duck to water. My mom and dad just kept signing me up for lessons. When I was old enough, I came out and started helping Bess. I was her stable boy first. I mucked out the stalls and fed the horses and saddled them up for tourists to ride. Then I moved up to leading the rides. I also worked at the resort like the rest of my family. But they knew I wasn't going to go into the resort business. None of the boys did. I'm glad my sisters wanted to carry on when Mom and Dad retired."

He led the way into the trees. As she followed, she found herself watching the strong, straight back of a man who knew how to ride. He carried himself well on the horse and she was intrigued by him. She wasn't sure how he was going to manage this place and his Texas ranch unless he found a manager for it.

"How many acres does this property have?" she asked.

"There's sixty. Not many according to Texas standards, but for beach property, it costs almost as much."

"I bet it does." There were trails all through the palm trees and green foliage. It was still untouched and rustic.

"Will you eventually sell the place?" she asked.

"This land won't be for sale. I have history here that I want to preserve for my kids one day."

Lana liked that. Her history ran deep in Texas and her dad had worked to preserve their heritage there. Her ancestor had first staked his claim on five thousand acres and that had grown through the years. Her dad planned on the land never being sold. It was still a working cattle ranch that had managed to survive. Oil had helped the ranch succeed when others struggled. And her dad had worked hard, as had his dad and granddad.

"You sure are quiet back there," Cam observed, shooting her a glance.

"Just thinking about roots. I've got them in Texas and though I'm here, I like knowing where I came from. I understand how you feel about this place."

"I thought you would."

When they reached the barns again, she dismounted and led her horse back to her stall. "I'll brush my horse down."

"You don't have to. I can do that for you."

She balked. "My dad would have my hide if I didn't. Besides, brushing down the horse is part of the experience."

"Go at it then." He narrowed his gaze. "So you really don't have a date for tonight?"

It made her feel better that his expression was one of disbelief.

"Yes, I do." She was unclenching the saddle as she spoke, and then tugged it from the horse and carried it over to the saddle rack.

"But you said you didn't get your date last night."

She placed her hands on her hips. "I could have gotten one through other means and not just buying a date at a bachelor auction."

He looked embarrassed. "Yes, you definitely could have done that."

"But I didn't. I have a date with a big box of Godiva and a movie to celebrate my single status. This time last year, I was mad as a hornet and using a certain cowboy as a target for hurling chocolate bon-bons at—even hit the bulls eye a few times... This year, I'm going to eat them and enjoy them."

He threw back his head and laughed. "I would've paid to see that."

"Well, let's just say I wish I had charged admission to it when he dared to set foot on my porch after I caught him at his cheating game. Chocolate-covered cherries work great for target practice. They make a lovely splatting sound on impact and the brown and red spots on a white dress shirt is art at its finest."

His eyes grew as wide as his grin. "I thought you said you didn't want to do anything like that."

"Sadly, that was what I did the night I discovered the truth. That was embarrassing enough and hard to live down. I didn't want to do anything more."

"He deserved it and it was cherries, not rocks."

"Yes, but would you want your child being taught at school by the teacher who lost control and did that?

Word got out and spread like wildfire. Social media is awful. I was blessed that it didn't go viral." And that was the truth.

"I get it. And I think you did good by refraining from any other retaliations. But still, he cheated on you with your best friend. Chocolate-covered cherries were a mild retribution, if you ask me. What did your dad and brothers do?"

"Oh, they wanted to do plenty, but it wasn't worth it. I suspect they warned him away from trying to get back at me because he didn't file charges."

"That's good at least." He scowled and then went to unsaddle his horse.

A few minutes later, he walked her to her truck. They'd struck up a friendship of sorts that was both unsettling for her and good for her. She had missed having conversations with a man. There was just something different about it than talking to girlfriends. And yet there was no denying the attraction she felt toward him and on that note, she was playing with fire. Because she was *not* going to date a cowboy.

"I'll see you later. This was great." She climbed

into her truck. Her heart thundered dangerously as she looked at him through the open window.

"Come back out later in the week," he invited as she cranked the truck.

"I might—"Her words halted when the battery just clicked.

He studied her skeptically. "You didn't get a new battery?"

She slapped the steering wheel. "No. I came to ride first and then was going to get one," she said, embarrassed by the ordeal.

"Come on, let's go."He strode away.

She climbed out of her truck. "Where are you going?"

"I'm taking you to town to get a battery and then I'll put it in."

She stopped following him. "No way. I'm not going to have you wasting your time doing that. If you'll just give me a jump…"

"Nope. We're getting a battery."

"Look, stop. I am not going to waste your time—"

He looked unfazed. "Stop arguing. I'd be wasting

my time charging this battery. Besides, I'm hungry and I don't have anything here to eat. I'll buy you lunch."

She frowned, and then her stomach growled loudly as if to give her incentive to agree. "Okay, let's do this then. But this is not your responsibility."

He strode toward his truck and she followed. They climbed inside the cab.

"I understand that. You've made that clear. We are just going to get you a battery and you're going to come along while I grab something to eat and so you might as well get something too. And then we'll quickly slip that battery into your truck and you can go home. Have your chocolate and enjoy your evening all by yourself."

The man was funny. He was making fun of her in a teasing way. "Thanks," she muttered. "You make it sound awful."

He laughed. "Yeah, well. I'll be here, having coffee and going over my boundary lines. I might have to get me some of that chocolate you were talking about and then I'll be having just as much fun as you are." He smiled. "But we are free."

It was her turn to laugh. "Yes, we are."

This had definitely not been the morning she had expected when she'd come to ride today. She was having a good time with him, like it or not it was a fact. But tonight she'd be doing exactly what she wanted and had planned for, eating chocolate and celebrating her single status. And forgetting last Valentine's Day fiasco. She smiled and rolled her window down to let the salty air inside.

"Yep, if your ex could see that twinkle in your eyes right now, I can guarantee you he'd be sorry."

"But I'm not. So all is good."*And you're having lunch with a very handsome cowboy.* Once more she reminded the irritating voice in her head that she wasn't ready for dating and never would be with a cowboy.

CHAPTER FOUR

Thirty minutes later, Cam placed the battery into the back of the truck and they climbed back into the cab."See, that wasn't so painful."

"Don't rub it in. I know I should have already done that."

"I can't help myself."

She just shook her head. The man was fun. And he had a sense of dry humor that she found somewhat similar to her brothers' and yet where they really got to her sometimes, she found Cam's dry humor fun. It was somewhat odd that she thought that way.

"There's a little beach restaurant down the road from here that serves up a great fish taco. Among other things, even a great burger. How does that sound for lunch?"

"I'm fine with that. Sounds a whole lot better than the ham sandwich I would've eaten if I'd gone home."

"Then Paradise Grill it is."

Two minutes later, he pulled into the parking lot of a faded blue wooden building with a thatch roof and doors that were open. The floors were wooden and ceiling fans overhead stirred the air around. The tables and booths were situated throughout the room, with a bar in the center of the room. It was busy for lunch. The back of the building was open and the beach was the view. Cam led the way out to the deck facing the beach area.

"Is this okay? We can eat inside if you'd rather."

Seagulls squawked in the distance and there were signs that warned to not feed the birds. A good idea to help keep the scavengers at a distance. "Oh, no. I love being on the beach. I can't seem to get enough of it."

She had not been here before but she already knew

she'd be back. She'd expected to just grab a burger at a fast-food restaurant, so this was a pleasant surprise. Cam didn't seem to be in any hurry, though. And that was something she hadn't expected. He had a lot to do and she knew that. And yet, he'd taken time out to help her and suddenly seemed as if he had all the time in the world for lunch. With her.

Several tables were filled and Cam glanced around to see whether there was anyone he recognized or whether the owner, Bert Zane, was around. He and Bert had gone to school together and when he'd opened this place several years ago, it had quickly become a great hangout.

"Hey, Sinclair."Bert came out from the inside of the grill. He held out his hand and Cam stood then clasped his hand. "Caught sight of you from the kitchen but I was putting out fires so couldn't get out here sooner. How's it going? We seem to be seeing a lot of you lately."

"Your burgers and fish tacos keep bringing me

back, man. I can't seem to leave them behind."

Bert laughed. He was a large guy, at least six foot five, and had been a linebacker through high school and college. He was now his own bouncer when nonsense broke out in the grill. But Cam and all his other friends knew the man had a heart of gold.

"I'm sure your family thanks me then for bringing you back to town."

They laughed and Cam looked at Lana. "This is Lana Presley. She's fairly new in town and didn't know about your place."

Bert held out a hand. "Welcome. I'll have to bring you a Hula pie on the house when you finish your meal. My welcome to you."

"I love your place. It's nice to meet you. And Hula pie sounds interesting. What is that?"

Cam smiled at Lana. "You'll love it. Lana is a schoolteacher down at the elementary school. First grade, I think, right?" She nodded. "She came out and rode at my new stable today."

Bert squinted at him. "Your stable? What did I miss in this conversation?"

Cam laughed. "I haven't even told my family, so don't mention it to anyone. I'll be telling them this afternoon. But I bought Bess's place. So you'll be seeing me often."

"Get outta here," Bert said. "You're moving back?"

"No, just bought the place. I'll have a manager."

"That's great, man. I wondered what was up with that place. I heard Bess had left town to hang with her sister on some cruises or something. But I thought she'd just closed the place up. Now I know. This is good. Your mom is going to be ecstatic."

"Yes, she is. But I'll still be in Texas for the majority of the time."

"I'm sure she'll take whatever she can get. Okay, I'll let you two get back to it. What can we get you for lunch?"

"The fish tacos," Cam said and Lana agreed. After Bert left, Cam focused on Lana. "Sorry about that. Bert's a great guy."

"He seems to be. Y'all go way back?"

"To high school. We all played football together."

She smiled and Cam found himself drawn to everything about Lana. Especially the twinkle in her eyes when she smiled. "I bet y'all had a football team much like my brothers. When there are five brothers close in age, you probably filled the line."

"There were several years where that was the case. Bert was a good one to have on the front line. We did pretty good through the years. But for the most part, it was a great bonding experience. The team likes to get together when they can. We have our own reunions. Usually here."

"That sounds like fun."

"It is." He wasn't interested in talking about his past, though. He wanted to know more about her. And it had been a very long time since he'd been so curious about a woman. But Lana Presley had his attention. His full attention.

Lana studied Cam sitting across from her on the deck. They'd just enjoyed the most delicious fish tacos she'd ever eaten. And now were waiting on the promised

Hula pie. Cam looked relaxed, despite the fact that he wore a t-shirt, jeans, and boots rather than shorts and flip-flops like most of the men roaming around the beach bar. She wore boots too, so it wasn't as if he were dressed any differently than she was. It was…what?

The fact that he didn't fit in here. He had been born here and raised here, but he looked as if he belonged on the range. And her pulse did a dangerous quickstep at that thought. His gaze met and held hers; he cocked his head slightly, giving her a sigh-worthy look.

"What are you so deep in thought about? Should I be worried?" He flashed a charmingly sexy smile at her.

"Oh, I was thinking that you really don't fit in with the beach tourist scene. I'd never guess you were raised here."

"Believe it or not, but I can fit in. I'm a chameleon."

She laughed. "You are a comedian, I think."

"So now you know my secret. I do stand up in my

spare time."

"Here you go."Bert broke into their conversation by suddenly appearing and setting a huge piece of ice cream pie topped with whipped cream and chocolate sauce between them. There were two spoons on the plate. "Enjoy the Hula pie for two."

Her mouth had started to water the moment he set the pie on the table. It looked amazing. "Thank you. You just sealed the deal on me being here at least once a week. Could do more often, but my hips would hate me."

"Your hips look fine, so eat up."Bert winked and then walked away.

"I think Bert's right. You look great. Enjoy."He picked up a spoon and waited for her to do the same. "Ladies first."

They were eating a dessert together. It was more like something one would do on a date and this was not a date, but what the heck. She dipped her spoon into the heavenly creation too ready to taste it to worry too much about anything else. It was rich and creamy— vanilla ice cream with graham cracker crust, whipped cream, and drizzled with chocolate. Cam hesitated as she took the bite. When the sweet taste hit her taste buds, she sighed and pointed her spoon at the dessert. "Oh. My. Oh my," she mumbled as the sweet vanilla and chocolate melted in her mouth.

She realized he was smiling and still not eating.

"You're missing out. Why aren't you eating?"

His brows quirked, his forehead wrinkled beneath his Stetson. "I don't know that I've ever seen it enjoyed that much."

She chuckled once again. It seemed they'd done a lot of that today. It felt great. "Eat. Either dig in or you'll miss out completely."

His lip hitched upward as he dug his spoon in and joined her.

Later, at the stables she climbed into her truck— new battery installed thanks to him—she lifted a hand in farewell. "I just have to say thanks for the morning and for the battery install. But mostly thanks for the pie. A-maz-*ing!*"

"I'm glad it was a good day. I enjoyed it. Funny, the difference a year can make in your life, isn't it? I hope you have a great evening. See you later."

She thought about that as she headed out of the drive. She was going home to eat her chocolate and enjoy a Valentine's Day evening alone. But what had been an awful day last year had been a great day this year. And much of that had to do with Cam Sinclair.

Not for romantic reasons, she clarified to herself. He'd just been a friend today. But as she settled on the couch with a small box of chocolate and turned on a romantic comedy, she couldn't help wondering what he was doing.

She pushed that thought right out of her mind and turned up the volume of the movie. Finally, thirty minutes later, uninterested and restless, she turned off the movie, closed her chocolate and walked to her small second bedroom in the house she was renting. She turned on the light and stared at the unfinished painting on the easel. Her thoughts whirled and she moved to the easel. *It was a good night to paint.*

Her paints were set up in this room that she used as a studio but they'd been sitting there, untouched for a few weeks because she'd felt stuck. She walked over and stared at the beach scene. Something had been missing and she'd just not been able to figure out what it was. Now, taking a brush out, she sank down onto the stool. She opened a few varied colored tubes of oil paint and squeezed it onto the tray. And then, she started to paint the horse she'd suddenly realized was missing from the scene.

She smiled as her brushstrokes began forming him. He was running, mane flowing in the breeze, sand and foam from the surf showing movement with each step of his hoof.

After an intense hour, she sat back and studied her creation. It was good. And that painting had sat there all this time, waiting for him to be placed where he belonged.

She'd tried hard to create something other than what she'd always loved to paint and that was horses. But that was because when she came here, she had been trying to break away from her roots in Texas. Her breakup had just torn at her soul and she'd been trying to deny everything about her life before. But now, that just seemed ridiculous. If she wanted to paint a horse, then she would. She had. And she loved it.

Time.

It had taken a year for that realization to come to her…or had it taken twenty-four hours from the moment she'd first met Cam Sinclair?

CHAPTER FIVE

On Monday, Lana walked into the classroom to find a smiling Jessica and a beaming Kevin.

"Miss Presley, Miss Presley, Levi is going to be my daddy," Kevin exclaimed, looking up from the desk where he was coloring a picture. They were often the only three in the classroom before the kids started to arrive and it was not uncommon for Kevin to be coloring to pass the time. But today he held up a picture and raced over to her. "See, I'm drawing a picture. That's me, my mom, Levi, and there's our dogs Jaco and Roscoe. We're a family."

Her heart swelled with happiness for Kevin. She glanced at Jessica, who had turned a fuchsia pink.

"I love it, Kevin. I think this is so cool. You should finish your picture. It's looking beautiful."

He beamed proudly and looked at the picture. "I'm going to finish it because I'm gonna give it to Levi tonight when he comes to our house."

Lana walked over and crossed her arms as she looked at Jessica. "So, Friday night was a really interesting evening. And I gather after you left the auction with Levi, things went well?"

Jessica chuckled. "They went so well. I should've called you. I'm sorry."

Lana held up her hands. "Oh no, I was hoping you were really busy. And I actually was busy too."

"We..."Jessica sighed. "We decided to get married."

Lana gaped at her. "Married? So Kevin isn't just saying Levi is going to be his daddy this time. This is quick, are you sure?"

"Well, yes." She leaned in close so that their voices were low. "I love him and was letting fear hold me back. He and I connected right away. And not that I'm comparing him to Adam, but that's how it was with him too. I dated a lot before I met Adam but I knew almost immediately that he was for me. And when he died, I just never thought it would be possible to feel this way about someone else. But I do. Levi is so wonderful. I was just denying it because of fear. And being worried for Kevin."

"I'm thrilled for you. I know you are very level-headed and everything I know about Levi says he's one of the most respected men in Windswept Bay. I'm really happy for you both."

"Would you be my maid of honor?"

A lump formed in her throat. They had formed a bond at the beginning of the school year, both of them having moved to Windswept Bay under similar circumstances, needing space in their lives from their families. They'd connected and been support for each other.

"Jessica, I would be so honored."Her voice cracked as she hugged her friend.

Tears glistened in Jessica's eyes. "Thank you. For

helping and for pushing me to take the step out of my comfort zone. You knew I needed to do it."

Lana smiled. "I felt like you just needed a little nudge."

"And what about you? Did you end up doing any bidding at the auction after I left with Levi?"

They were already speaking softly so Kevin wouldn't hear but now Lana spoke softer. "Nope, I sure didn't. I'm not interested. I haven't been completely honest with you. I went through a really terrible breakup before I moved here. I thought the guy was going to propose to me when he was actually having an affair with my best friend. And I was the talk of the town. I got tired of that and my family worrying me to death. So that's the whole story to how I got here."

"I thought there was more to that story. What a jerk. I would have probably had to move or I would have found him in a coffee shop and poured coffee on his head."

Lana laughed. "Actually, that was one of the reasons I left—because I was afraid I *would* do that."

She had thrown chocolate after all.

"I guess that wouldn't have gone down very well in town for the first grade teacher to be retaliating like that," Jessica said, softly.

"I didn't think it would. So I took the temptation away and moved here."The bell rang. "Okay, anyway, I wanted to tell you that I met Levi's brother after the auction."

"Which one?"

"Cam, the cowboy."

"Oh, *really*." Kids started coming into the room. "I need to know all about it."

"Sure. He bought the horse stable in town. He was telling his family yesterday."

"Yes, Levi called and told me that. So, did you like him? I've met him and thought you two might hit it off."

"I went riding at the stables yesterday. But I'm not looking for a cowboy when I start dating. He does seem like a really nice guy, though."

"So are we going to become sisters-in-law?"

Lana rolled her eyes. "Don't get your hopes up.

Like I said, I'm off the market right now and especially when it comes to cowboys. I'm going to marry an accountant or a football coach. Not a cowboy."

"Ha. Something tells me that's not true."Jessica smiled and then turned to address the room of kids. Then she looked over her shoulder at Lana. "Oh, by the way, he's going to be Levi's best man, so you'll be spending a little time with him. So my dream of being your sister-in-law could come true."

Lana shook her head. "I can spend time with him. I'm not marrying him," she warned and headed back to her desk and to her kids, who were settling into their seats.

She was not marrying the man. She could spend time with him and enjoy herself. But she was not marrying anyone.

Still, she couldn't deny that the idea of seeing him again made her smile.

Cam stared at all of his brothers. They'd all met at Jake's dive shop and sat around on the back deck, watching the boats on the dock. Trent and Levi were twins but he and Levi had always been closer. Jake and Trent had hung out together more growing up and both loved diving. Jake's hair was still damp after having come in from a dive. Levi had called the meeting and everyone but Max had made it. He had left the night of the bachelor auction and gone on a mission. They never knew how long he'd be gone as a Navy SEAL Special Ops and they were always glad when he made it home.

He'd told Levi earlier and been surprised that Cali or Grant hadn't mentioned it to the other brothers and sisters. But as far as he knew none of the others knew his news. But Levi had news of his own.

"So what's up, Levi?"Jake looked expectantly at the chief of police of Windswept Bay. They all had an idea what he was about to say.

"No, I want to hear what's going on with Cam first."

"You're stalling."

Levi chuckled. "No, I want the spotlight."

"Oh, then that's better. I told Mom and Dad

yesterday that I bought Bess's stables so I thought y'all might already know."

"No kidding. Nope, I didn't know." Jake looked startled. "You always did love that place. But how'll you manage it and your ranch in Texas?"

"Yeah," Trent said. "It's a great idea but you live in Texas."

Levi hitched a brow. "I know you have a plan. You always have a plan."

Cam tilted his Stetson back on his forehead. "I have a gal coming to run it for me. She's working at a ranch near Orlando, where I've bought stock. She's looking for change. I heard that there was a little trouble where she was at and contacted her. She has a great reputation, so the place will be in great hands."

"So a woman?" Trent asked. "Sounds interesting."

"She's nice but knows her mind. She'll do good. So, Levi, what's your news?" he asked, knowing what was coming.

Levi grinned. "I thought you'd never ask. I'm getting married, guys."

None of his brothers looked surprised. Jake

crossed his arms and cocked his head to the side. "Are we supposed to be surprised? You were one lovesick puppy the other night at the auction. Congratulations."

Trent was grinning and so was Cam as they joined in on the congratulations.

"I've asked Cam to be my best man but want all of you to stand up with me. Max too."

Everyone agreed and Cam looked around the group. This was his roots. He was happier now than ever that he'd bought Bess's place. "So when are you going to bring them out to ride?"

"Hey, that's a great idea. Kevin would love it. I'll see when they can come out and let you know."

"Sounds good. Speaking of Saturday night, how did the Valentine dates go?"

"I had a nice time," Trent said. "My date and I agreed that it was for charity and we had a nice dinner and that's about it."

Jake grinned. "I have another date Saturday night."

That drew laughs from everyone.

Cam said, "Why are we not surprised?"

"Hey, she was nice. We get along." Jake grinned.

If Jake ever fell for a woman, she'd have to be far more than nice. He thought all females were nice. Cam wasn't going to hold his breath for Jake to settle down. Levi hadn't surprised him. And he could see Trent settling down in the near future but Max and Jake were different. Max had a very unsettled life. And Jake…he enjoyed being single.

He left a little while later and hadn't mentioned to anyone that he'd met Lana in the parking lot. He would have had to answer questions if he'd done that. And he wasn't sure how to answer questions about Lana. They'd just met but he'd had her on his mind ever since she'd driven off on Saturday.

He'd spent Valentine's Day evening looking over the books for the stables and had to force himself to concentrate because he kept thinking about her.

She knew Jessica, so maybe he'd invite her out the day Levi brought Jessica and Kevin out. Good idea…

He wondered what she would think if he called her up.

He almost called her but decided that would

probably make her think he was a fast mover and he had a feeling that was the last thing she was looking for. No, going slow was the best thing he needed to do where she was concerned. So he kept his fingers off the phone and on the paperwork he was going over and spent a quiet Valentine's Day evening alone.

But he wanted to go faster.

On Tuesday afternoon, Lana walked out of the school and headed toward her truck. Her footsteps slowed as she saw a certain good-looking cowboy leaning against her truck: boots crossed, cowboy hat pushed back, arms crossed. *He was waiting on her.* Instantly, her heart beat rapidly and butterflies fluttered through her chest.

"Hey, you get lost?" she asked, fighting the sensations fluttering through her.

A slow smile spread across his face and his navy eyes studied her. "I don't have your phone number and I don't have your address. But I knew where you worked and what your truck looks like, so here I am."

"Yes, here you are." She mused. Drinking him in like cool sweet tea.

"I thought I'd just swing by and see if maybe you were up for a horse ride?"

"Really?" More flutters—drat those butterflies.

"Yeah. I've got something to show you. I thought you might enjoy it. But if you have school papers or something to grade, I understand."

That made her smile more. "It's first grade. We don't give homework too often. I'm curious, what do you want to show me?"

He grinned. "Nope, not telling. This is a show-and-tell. I think you know what that is."

"Oh, do I ever." She chuckled. "Okay, you've got my curiosity. I need to swing by the house and put on my boots and then I'll come out."

"How about I follow you? Then you can ride with me and I'll bring you back to your house when we're done."

"I can drive my truck."

"I guess, if you insist, that'll be fine. I'll still follow and wait for you."

"Okay then, come on. I'll change and let you carry me out there if that's what you want to do."

A few minutes later, she pulled into the drive of her bungalow and he pulled his big truck in behind her. She hopped out of her truck; he exited his truck and came toward her.

"I like your place." He studied the yellow cottage with the white trim. "It's very beachy. Nobody would know you were from Texas or a cowgirl."

She hitched a brow. "I'm in transition. I left my cowgirl behind. Or at least, some of her."

He shook his head. "No, she's right here. I'm looking at her."

"Hey, you left your beach guy behind and went Texas cowboy."

"I did but no matter whether my heart is in Texas or not, my roots are here in Florida with my family. And yours is back there in Texas with your family. That jerk can't take your roots from you."

She put her hands on her hips. "Tell me what you really think."

He laughed. "I will. Always, Miss Feisty. Now,

come on, daylight is burning. Grab those boots. And probably an old shirt just in case."

She stopped in her tracks and her mouth fell open."The mare is having her foal."

He grinned. "Are you trying to mess up my surprise?"

Her eyes narrowed. "Why didn't you already say so? We've wasted all this time! Hold on. I'll be right out." She spun and ran toward her house.

He followed."I figured you were the only person I knew around here who would appreciate what's about to happen like I will."

It had been so long since she had witnessed the birth of a foal and the very idea tickled her. There was nothing like it. Except a sweet child being born.

She hurried through the house and heard him follow her inside. "I'll be right out," she called and headed toward her room. Within five minutes, she had her boots on and she had changed into a denim shirt that she hadn't worn in a while. As an afterthought, she reached up onto her closet shelf and pulled out her cowboy hat. She stared at it for a moment. *Was he right about her roots?*

He was studying photos on the entrance table when she came around the corner. He held up one of her dad and her brothers when they were younger.

"I can see why you felt a little intimidated."

She laughed. In the picture, she stood at the center of her five older brothers and her dad. Being the youngest, she looked dwarfed by them.

"Yes, that photo says it all. It was tough for anybody to get up the nerve to ask me out. You can only imagine. They might not be holding a shotgun but all the fellas knew they owned them."

"I figure they were holding them behind their backs."He grinned and set the picture back down."It might be late when this is over, so I'd rather bring you home than have you be tired and drive."

She shrugged."Okay." She could hear her dad applauding everything Cam had proposed. He'd have been pleased. *She needed to give her dad a call.* She might do that tomorrow.

When Cameron realized the mare was going to give birth, he'd known Lana would want to be there.

And he'd wanted to share it with her. Plus, she had offered to help if he needed it. He didn't but he did want to see her again and this was the perfect excuse.

The mare was still on her feet but very restless when they got back to the stables.

"She's a beautiful mare. I can't wait to see what the foal looks like. My gut tells me she's having a colt."

"And is your gut good at knowing?"

They stood at the stall gate, their elbows hanging over the top of it. She glanced up at him; her shoulder brushed his and he couldn't help but feel his blood humming at the thought of being so close to her.

So sue him—he was attracted to her.

He couldn't help himself. Her clear green eyes were mesmerizing. Her intelligence and her wit were alluring. And her determination and stubbornness made him smile. Everything about her attracted him.

"I get it right about fifty percent of the time." She winked.

He chuckled, not wanting to disturb the mare. "You're that good?"

"Oh yeah. I'm going to guess this is a colt and we will see if my fifty-fifty chance holds true."

She was funny. "I'm not going to bet against you, because I have a feeling that the odds are with you."

"You're as smart as I thought you were. So I hear you're going to be best man at Levi and Jessica's wedding. I'm going to be maid of honor."

"I heard that. So I guess that means we might have to help make a few decisions?"

"Maybe, but I don't think it's going to be a big wedding, so there may not be any decisions to make, other than helping figure out where she's going to have a bachelorette party. And you probably help Levi to figure out where to have his bachelor party."

"I'm not thinking they're going to be into that too much. Levi couldn't care less about a bachelor party. I haven't met Jessica yet, but from what I heard of her, I wasn't thinking she'd be much into the bachelorette party thing."

"I think you're right."

"Maybe they'd want to go have a party together with the wedding party, I mean, you know—combine their bachelorette and bachelor party together?"

"You know, you are smart. I bet Jessica would love that. I will ask her about it tomorrow."

Cam patted himself on the back. It would mean spending more time with Lana while celebrating with Levi. He grinned. "Sounds good."

The horse snorted, pawed at the hay and then lay down in the hay.

Lana's eyes grew bright. "Oh, here we go," she whispered in awe and placed her hand on his arm.

Instant awareness radiated through him and he had a hard time thinking about the imminent birth as every cell in his body tuned into Lana.

"We should go inside. She might need help."Lana reached for the latch. He stepped back to let her open the gate and then followed her inside. She knelt at the mare's head and spoke soothingly to the horse as she gently rubbed a hand down its neck.

"You're doing great, girl."

He watched the expression on Lana's face, and felt like she was feeling the same great joy, giving comfort to the mare. He liked that about her. He liked everything about her.

The birth went without a hitch. The baby colt was born within the hour and Lana was thrilled as she watched the baby try to stand.

"Come on, sweet boy, you can do it," she urged from the stall gate where they'd moved back to after the birth was over. "He's beautiful."

"Yes, he is. And your record holds."

She smiled. "I'm glad."

He laid his hand on her shoulder and brought her in to his side, giving her a tentative hug. "Thank you for sharing this with me."

She was startled by the move but they'd just experienced something beautiful and they'd bonded in a way. She looked up at him."I wouldn't have missed it. Thanks for thinking of me."

Their gazes held and she got the feeling he was thinking about kissing her. The thought shot her pulse flying. Everywhere their bodies were touching hummed. She almost tipped her head toward him.

The gentle nicker of the mare pulled her attention back to the colt. He was attempting a wobbly rise to stand. "Here goes." She grabbed Cam's hand that was resting on her shoulder. The newborn golden-toned palomino got shakily to its feet. It stood awkwardly, its knees shaking. His mother nudged him gently along, giving him encouragement with her nose.

"He's beautiful," she said softly.

"You are too."

She looked up, startled by his words. But more startled by the pleasure curling through her because of his words.

CHAPTER SIX

Cam couldn't help being honest in that moment. Maybe it was the man in him or the fact that he had seen a lot of baby colts standup, but all his attention was focused on Lana.

All he could say was her ex was a fool. And for her to have left her home and moved all the way to Windswept Bay, she must have been hurt deeply. Must have loved the guy like crazy.

And the fool had thrown that away. Cam had known her five days and he couldn't understand how something so precious could have been tossed like that.

He swallowed hard and fought the tidal wave of emotions swallowing him up.

She turned her face toward his; her eyes suddenly softened and looked vulnerable.

"You are beautiful, you know," he said softly. Then, unable—or not willing—to stop himself, he kissed her.

She stilled for a second and then her hand went to his chest and she came into the kiss.

Moments stopped. His heart pounded as he lifted his head and stared into her slightly dazed eyes. He had a feeling he looked the same way.

"I think we have a problem," he gritted through a clenched jaw.

"Un-huh." She sighed. "I don't date cowboys."

"Exactly," he muttered and then pulled her back for another kiss.

Everything was spinning as Lana wrapped her arms around Cam's neck and returned the kiss.

They'd just shared a wonderful experience in

helping birth the colt and she'd been so aware of him throughout the event that her defenses were weakened. She was so attracted to him, far beyond anything she had ever felt before, and watching his gentleness with the mare had only made her like him more.

She needed to back out of his embrace, break the kiss, put distance between them—but her dusty boots seemed cemented to the floor of the stable.

Instead, she wrapped her arms around him and gave into the joy of the kiss.

But she didn't date cowboys. They were just trouble where her love life was concerned.

She had to not let herself be influenced…She mustered determination and stepped back, breaking the kiss.

Cam immediately released her but his gaze was clouded."I hope you reconsider your position on cowboys," he said, huskily.

She groaned silently. "I honestly don't know what to say, Cam. This is all a surprise…I need some space. Clearly we are attracted to each other but that doesn't mean it's good for me. I'm attracted to sugar too, but I try to avoid it."

He frowned and she didn't blame him. "That guy really hurt you, didn't he?"

She nodded. "It makes me mad that he had that much power over me…and I just can't do it again."

"I'm not happy about it, but I understand."

Why was this so hard?"So, what will you do with the foal?" she asked, needing to move on.

His eyes were shuttered and he studied her, probably trying to decide whether she was seriously just going to move forward.

The man had just kissed her boots off and she was pretending she was unaffected.

"I'm going to take the mare and the colt back to my ranch in Texas. I want my trainer to look at it. I do that with all my newborns."

She'd struggled to ignore how much she wanted to step back into his arms. Wanted to feel his lips on hers again and the strength of his arms around her. How much she already missed the beat of his heart against hers and the roughness of his five o'clock shadow bristling against her skin.

What was wrong with her? She shivered, thinking about his touch and the passion of his kiss. *And the promise of it.* But she knew promises could be empty, and touches and kisses could be deceptive.

She did not need a cowboy. She nodded at him. She turned to face the colt again. "When will you travel?"

"Probably this weekend. My new stable manager is coming tomorrow. I'll show her what needs to be done and then I'll head out."

Lana took a deep breath."When will you be back?"

"Not sure. Is it going to bother you?"

Her fingers gripped the gate. She closed her eyes for a moment before she looked back at him."No. You have to do what you have to do. You're only here temporarily."

He nodded. "I'll be back. We have a wedding to plan."

"Right. I probably need to be getting home."

He nodded. His jaw was tight and she figured he was probably reevaluating why he'd kissed her.

"Lead the way to the truck," he said.

The atmosphere was strained as he drove and she sat in the passenger side, contemplating her options. She was passing on something she shouldn't and yet memories of a year ago jumped vividly to her mind.

Relationships with cowboys had just never worked for her, even before the jerk. None of those relationships had worked out—sure, common sense would say they weren't the right one for her, but still, if you kept going down the same road over and over again, refusing to make a change, then how could you ever change the course of bad decisions?

To get a different result meant she needed to make a major change, which she had done by moving to Windswept Bay and making the decision not to date cowboys any more.

And she would stick to her guns on this. *So why did it feel so lousy?*

As soon as they got to her house, she got out of the truck.

He followed her and walked her to her door. She wished he'd stayed in the truck so as not to tempt her with wanting another kiss. "I'll see you when I get back. And we'll plan the party," he said. "I'll talk to Levi about that in the morning."

She'd forgotten about the party. "Right—the party, yes. I'll mention it to Jessica."

He nodded and then, as her chest ached, he surprised her with a quick kiss to the cheek. Just a barely there brush of his lips to her skin and then he was striding away, back to his truck, one long-legged stride at a time. Leaving her wanting more. Drat the man.

Lana couldn't move as she watched him stride away. *Was she watching the best thing ever in her life walk away?*

Cam forced himself to keep walking, to not look back, to not storm back and sweep Lana into his arms and kiss her like he wanted to. But he felt as though he were gentling a skittish horse when he was around her. She definitely wasn't a horse, but she wasn't trusting at all. And she was always ready to run.

He'd messed up when he'd kissed her.

Now, he was going to pull back, try to give her time to forgive him for acting so impulsively and ruining a great evening and possibly ruining any chance at all that he might have had with Lana. His mood wasn't improved by the time he got back to the stable. Stalking straight inside, he saddled the black gelding. The horse studied him as he set the saddle blanket on its back and then the saddle.

"Yes, we are going for a ride in the dark," Cam grunted as he cinched the saddle and secured it.

Moments later, the moonlight cast a golden spotlight on the dark waters as he let his horse lope along the shoreline. With the cool night's breeze and the hum of the surf shimmering with moonlight, he knew it was going to be the perfect night for a romantic ride...only he was alone and thinking of Lana.

How had his feelings for her moved so quickly? He was normally a very methodical thinker. A man who didn't make snap decisions, who looked at all aspects of a big move and then proceeded. He was not a man who made rash decisions or fell easily for anything. What he felt for Lana might be sudden but it wasn't rash. Something about her spoke to him. And he wasn't giving up on her.

He brought his horse to a halt. *No, he would just step back and then he'd move with caution.* He'd win her over slowly, giving her wounded heart time to open up.

The next day came slowly. Lana had spent most of the night up and down pacing, trying to read, trying to paint…basically fighting the urge to call Cam and say she hadn't meant what she'd said.

But she had meant it.

Being raised by her dad and her brothers, she'd had to be tough like all the guys. And when she'd suffered the worst hurt and betrayal of her life, she'd held it in as much as possible. But that had only made it worse…it had festered and now no matter how wonderful and amazing she'd felt in Cam's arms, the pain of last year surged up and tore the goodness away.

She just didn't know whether she could ever trust anyone with her heart again. His kiss had been heaven on earth. Just the thought of it right now sent chills and thrills racing through her. And that was scary because…*why?*

She thought about that for a moment. *Because she didn't trust herself anymore.*

Exactly. She'd fallen for similar feelings of passion before—how could she know this was different?

She couldn't.

"You look glum this morning," Jessica said in greeting as she joined her for morning drop-off duty.

"Thanks, it's called a sleepless night," she grunted and held up a paper cup of coffee. "I just need a little more of this and all this nice fresh air and I'll be fine in a few minutes." She yawned. "Just starting off slow."

They moved to help kids out of cars. A few minutes later, as they headed back inside toward their room, Lana decided now was the best time to ask, despite the fact that when she asked the question Jessica would know she'd spent time with Cam and that might get her friend asking questions again.

"Are you planning on having a bachelorette party?"

A bubble of laughter erupted from Jessica instantly. "No, I certainly am not. I'm too settled for that, and I had one when Adam and I got married—we girls had an evening at a spa, getting pampered."

"That sounds fun. Cam and I talked, and he said Levi wouldn't want a bachelor party so he suggested combining the bachelorette party with the bachelor party at a local gathering place for an enjoyable evening."

"I think that would be a really good idea," Jessica said. "I'm still shocked that we are actually talking about my wedding."

"Have you set a date yet?"

"Three weeks. My family is coming. And that gives them time to get here." Jessica blushed.

"That's wonderful! Three weeks, wow." Lana was a little shocked at the speed. "So they're okay with how fast it's happened?"

"They are so excited but yes, a bit worried about

how quickly it's happened. But they don't really have a say and I think they get that now. I think the most shock is realizing I'll be settling here in Windswept Bay. They can't believe it. Deep down they hoped I would be coming home."

Jessica knew that was what her dad hoped. "I think that's normal. I know my dad thinks I'll come back to Texas. And my brothers—they're all in denial that I even moved."

Jessica studied her. "Are you sure you want to stay here? I mean, you said you enjoyed going out to ride…maybe you're starting to miss home."

"I had a great time and will admit that I have started lately to think about home more. But I love paradise too. Windswept Bay is wonderful. I have a place to go and ride now, so all is good."

"I want to go out there. Maybe you could teach Kevin how to ride at the stable?"

"I'd love to give him some lessons. We'd have to talk to Cam about it. I was actually out there last night. Cam invited me to witness a mare giving birth. I love watching new babies."

"I bet that was amazing. You're a cowgirl, Lana—there is no getting away from who you are."

Lana told her about the baby but she didn't tell her about the kiss. Jessica would urge her to go for it—after all, that's what she'd told Jessica to do.

"Oh, Kevin would love seeing the new colt. Take us out there this afternoon!"

Lana wanted to say no, but Cam was taking the baby back to Texas on the weekend so she knew the window of opportunity for Kevin to see the pretty newborn was short. "You don't need me to go out there. The two of you can go or get Levi to take you."

Jessica pulled out her phone and held up a hand. "I'll call Levi right now. I think he's off this afternoon but you need to come too and we can discuss the party together. Perfect idea."

Lana cringed. *Shoot.* She watched as Jessica smiled as the phone was obviously answered on the other end. She blushed slightly.

Lana loved watching her friend look happy. But she did not love the idea of having to go out there to the stable and seeing Cam so soon after they'd parted on strained terms.

"Okay, we're all set. We will go right after school. Levi thinks it's a great idea. He'll meet us here at the school and drive us all out there."

"Great."Lana forced a smile that did not reach farther than her lips. *Should she tell Jessica what had happened?* Maybe, but she couldn't. She just couldn't.

CHAPTER SEVEN

When school was over, sure enough, there sat Levi, waiting on them. Kevin was over-the-moon happy as he climbed into the backseat and Jessica climbed into the front seat.

"I'll take my truck and follow you," Lana said, thinking that maybe—just maybe—it would break down on the way. It had been acting up even though they had replaced the battery. She feared she was going to have to take it to the shop.

"If you're sure," Levi said. "That's probably a good idea just in case you want to stay longer than we do."

Was there a hint of something in his voice? Did Levi know that she had kissed his brother? Maybe she was just being paranoid.

Moments later, she pulled into the yard behind Levi's truck. Sadly her vehicle had held up and she hadn't been stranded in five o'clock traffic.

Cam stood near the barn, talking to a tall, lean woman with thick blonde hair that was braided down the middle of her back. Instant jealousy rolled through Lana.

Who was this?

None of your business. The answer came back instantly. She had no claim on Cam. He could spend time with anyone he wanted to, even a beautiful blonde wearing tight jeans, a pretty lavender tank top, and boots. As Levi and Jessica got out of the truck and Kevin hopped from the backseat bubbling with excitement, Lana held back and moved a bit slower. She felt torn about being here. She would see the baby and make sure it was doing good. She would show him to Kevin and then she was out of here and going straight home.

Cam and the woman came toward them and Lana's pulse kicked up a storm.

"Hey, I'm glad y'all came out," he said, sounding every bit a born and bred Texan. "I'm glad you called me, Levi. Kevin, I'm Cam. Do you remember me from the birthday party at my mom's house?"

Kevin grinned and nodded.

Lana hadn't been at the party but she'd heard all about it from Jessica the next day.

"I remember you but I didn't know that you had a horse place. This is cool. Lana told me you had a baby horse."

Cam chuckled and his gaze met Lana's and held before sliding away after a couple seconds later. "This is called a stable. And Lana helped with the birth of this baby last night. She did an amazing job."

Kevin's eyes were huge. "Can I see? Can I see it?"The little boy jumped from foot to foot.

Everybody laughed at the kid's antics, so excited to see the new baby.

Lana remembered that feeling all too well. She

remembered going with her brothers and her dad the first time to the stalls to watch a baby being born. She remembered how cool it had felt. She couldn't even count how many colts and fillies she had helped bring into this world after that. Now, despite the misgivings rolling through her about Cam, she was excited about seeing the baby again one more time before it left for his ranch.

"She's in that stable right there, first stall."Cam looked at Levi and Jessica."This is Kelsey Malone. She's going to be running the place for me." His gaze met Lana's. "Kelsey, this is Lana, my friend. And this is Jessica, Levi's fiancée, and Levi is my brother."

So this was the girl or woman who would be running the place.

Jessica and Levi shook her hand and they all chitchatted as they followed Kevin toward the stables.

Kelsey held out her hand and smiled."It's nice to meet you. You did a great job helping with that baby. He's in really good shape. I'm familiar with your family's ranch. I think I know your brother, Vance."

"Oh, really?"

"Yes, I met Vance at the National Rodeo Finals last year. He went out with my roommate one night after their events."

"Small world, especially in the world of the NFR." To make it to the top championship took crisscrossing the country competing in rodeos and racking up points to qualify. Not everyone had the funds nor talent to manage it…her brother Vance had been on the road consistently until he got hurt last year and had to lay out for a while.

"Yes it is," Kelsey agreed.

"What did you compete in?"

"Barrels. I love them. We're thinking of even offering lessons here."

Lana did not know what to think about the emotions churning inside her. *Nothing—that's what she would do.* Pushing her shoulders back and putting her guard up, she knew with total conviction that she was not ready for a relationship.

This was ridiculous.

The man had kissed her; she had no claim on him.

"I see him," Kevin called, his words broke into her thoughts.

"Be easy as you go up to the gate," Cam warned.

"I will. I don't want to scare it," Kevin said, excitement written all over him.

The colt was adorable as it nursed from its mom. When they approached, it stopped nursing and looked at them curiously.

Kevin slowly, carefully stuck his hand through the gate and held it out to the baby, which looked at the hand with curiosity.

"Is it okay for him to do that?" Jessica looked from Cam to Lana.

Lana smiled and nodded and then looked at Cam, who also nodded.

"You're doing fine," Cam said and she liked the kindness she heard in his voice. "He's a little skittish, but I've tried to spend some time with it and it's not too scared right now."

And sure enough, about that time, the cute little fellow walked over and planted his muzzle right in

Kevin's palm. Kevin giggled. "He likes me. I want to learn to ride." He looked up at his mom and then Levi.

"I think that's a great idea," Jessica said, a look of delight on her face. "Do you think it will be possible to get lessons?"

Cam nodded. "It would be very possible. Kelsey will be giving lessons or if Lana wanted to teach him, she's more than welcome to come out here and use the horses." His gaze rested on her; butterflies scattered like geese inside her chest.

"We'll see. That would give me a chance to ride too but if you would rather Kelsey do it, that's fine. I wouldn't want to get in anybody's way."

Kelsey stuffed her hands on her slim hips and shook her head. "Oh no, believe me, it wouldn't step on my toes. There will be plenty of kids coming out here to have lessons, so I'm sure I'll have my hands full. If we take this to the next level like we've been discussing today, then I probably will even have to hire someone to help me teach the kids, if that's something you might be interested in. Cam told me you were a great horsewoman."

He'd been talking about her to Kelsey. "Thanks, but with my teaching, I couldn't possibly take on more than Kevin and maybe Jessica if she wants a few lessons."

Levi wrapped an arm around Jessica's shoulders. "That's a great idea. Kevin will love learning but you might want to learn to ride also."

"I would love to try." Jessica smiled.

"Yes, Momma, we'll learn together." Kevin raced over and threw his arms around her waist.

"It's going to be so fun." Jessica laughed and hugged him back. Lana and Kelsey laughed too.

"This was a great idea that you had, buying this place. Keeping Bess's dream going, plus it's good for the community."

"That's what I'm hoping," Cam said. "We're going to expand it, I think—do some different things that Bess has never done. I think we'll do some training. Kelsey's really good at what she does and I'm lucky to have her come on board to help me since I'll be in Texas the majority of the time." His gaze met Lana's.

Relief like a sweet breeze hit Lana—there didn't seem to be anything between him and Kelsey. *Although, who was to say something couldn't develop?* Lana reeled her imagination in. Her phone rang, giving her a much-needed distraction.

She pulled it out of her pocket and glanced at the ID. It was her brother, Drake. "I need to take this, excuse me." She walked away and answered the call.

"Hi. I was surprised to see your name on my phone." She smiled, though he couldn't see her. "It's good to hear from you."

"Lana, it's been too long, way too long."He sounded strained and she stiffened, wondering what was up. "I'm ready to see you but not this way. I'm afraid I've got some bad news—not as bad as it could have been though—praise God."

Fear gripped Lana. This was so not like Drake. "What's going on?"

"It's Dad. He's had a heart attack. He's stable, though."

The world swam and she sank to a feed box next to her. "How bad?" she managed as fear made it hard to breathe.

"Right now he's in ICU. He has great doctors and they have him stable. Thankfully he made it through without major damage. They're about to take him in and place a stent. But they'll do that laparoscopically—no open heart surgery."

"They're taking him in right now?"Lana couldn't breathe. "I'm on my way. Hurry, tell him before he goes in that I'm coming and that I love him."

"They've already taken him in. But he knows you love him. He'll be glad to see you when he wakes up, sis."

Tears filled her eyes and she could only nod as emotion clogged her throat.

"Like I said, he's stable. He's been having some problems that he did not tell us about. He's too tough to die, though, you know that." She heard the smile in Drake's voice. He was trying to make her smile. And they'd always thought their dad was invincible.

She'd believed that, but the truth was everybody had their moment.

"Are you okay?" Cam asked. He'd come to stand beside her and she looked up at him. She swiped at tears and he dropped to a knee beside her. "What's wrong?"

Her heart ached more at his obvious concern.

"You're pale as a sheet."

"Drake, let me get started. I'll talk to you soon."

"Sounds good."He said good-bye and she pulled the phone away.

"It's my dad—he's in ICU. He's had a heart attack and they're about to place a stent in his artery. I need to get to him."

The others gathered around and told her how sorry they were. They all tried to comfort her but it was hard to feel comfort when her dad was so far away.

"I'll take care of getting you a sub and letting the school know," Jessica said. "We need to get you a plane ticket." Jessica knelt beside her too.

"No, I'll drive. I'm embarrassed to tell you but, I have a horrible fear of flying. I can't do it. If I leave now, I mean as soon as I get home and pack a bag, I can get started. If I drive all night, I can be there by tomorrow."

"No, I'll drive you," Cam said. "You're in no condition to drive. Jessica and Levi, take her home and help her get her bags packed. I'll get the horses loaded and ready, and we'll head out as soon as I get there to pick her up."

"That's a great idea, Cam," Levi said. "She definitely doesn't need to drive."

"I can drive."

"I'm driving you and that's final." Cam stared at her. "Your dad's place is only about three hours from mine. I'll take you."

They sounded just like her brothers and her dad, taking charge. Any other time, Lana would have argued but right now she couldn't. "Thank you. I really appreciate it."

"Come on," Jessica said.

And looking solemn and older than his six years, Kevin came and put his little hand in hers. "Come on, we will help you," he said. "It's going to be all right."

"You are such a sweetheart." She stood.

"I'll take care of things here," Kelsey said. "Don't worry about that, Cam. Is there anything I can do for you, Lana?"

"No, but thank you." She was nice and Lana felt bad for having been jealous. The thought seemed out of place under the circumstances but still it was there.

Her thoughts were filled with worry as they traveled to her house. It was still sinking in that her dad really had a heart attack. It was just too hard to believe. She was in denial and she knew it.

She was grateful to Cam, though. The thought of driving all the way back to Texas by herself, when she was feeling so shaken—it would have been a hard drive. But Cam had taken charge and in this instance she was appreciative.

The man had readily jumped in and now she didn't have to face the drive alone. Didn't have to face the long, silent car ride with only her regrets and guilt to think about.

But now she'd have Cam to talk to. To distract her. Her dad would approve. Cam was her dad's kind of man.

The thought made her smile. She needed to see her dad.

Once home, she quickly threw together a suitcase full of clothes. Levi entertained Kevin in the living room. While Jessica helped her get her things together, her friend chattered up a storm, probably trying to distract her from worrying about her dad.

"Cam will take care of you and I'm so glad you're letting him do this. There's no way that you need to drive right now. And I had no idea you were terrified of flying. I would've never ever have guessed that about you, Lana. You're the type of person that I would think could do anything."

Lana took a deep breath. "Having a weakness like that drives me crazy but I haven't been able to overcome it. Surely if my brother had said, *Dad's dying; get on a plane and get here*—I would have been able to do it. Right?" The uncertainty made her sick to her stomach. Made her feel horrible.

"Yes," Jessica said instantly. "Stop worrying. If it was like that, you are strong enough and care enough for your dad that you would have overcome your fear and gotten on that plane. No doubt about it."

Lana felt as if she would have but even hesitating felt awful. "I don't like having a weakness. And I don't often show that I have them. Being raised by my dad and my brothers on the ranch, I was always trying to be as good and tough as all of them. Plus, I looked up to all my brothers and they treated me like the baby sister that I was. But that just made me try harder to be as tough as they were. But when it came to getting on a plane to fly, there was no pretending. Thank goodness when you're traveling to and from horse shows or rodeos you're hauling livestock of some sort, so traveling by truck was our main mode of transportation."

"Well, if it's any consolation, by the time you pack your suitcase and drive to the airport, wait for two hours before the flight—like they advise these days—and then land, grab your bags and drive from the airport to the hospital, you would have used six or seven hours up, maybe eight since you said the airport is a good two-hour drive from the hospital he's in. That could be ten hours. You may be able to make this drive in sixteen hours driving straight through…that's not too much difference. So that's encouraging."

Lana loved Jessica for trying so hard to make her feel better. But deep down, even knowing it wasn't that much longer of a time frame didn't help the guilt hanging over her.

Still, for Jessica, she said, "You're right. Thanks." She pushed the pain deeper inside and held it off…but it was there, pushing to break through the thin layer of her emotions.

The sound of the truck could be heard. "That must be Cam. I think I hear the rattle of the trailer."She grabbed her bag and followed Jessica out of her bedroom and headed toward the front door. Levi and Kevin were already on the porch.

Cam strode up the driveway. The truck and trailer were parked on the street in front of the house. As unlikely a time as this, her heart still skipped a beat and her stomach felt bottomless as she watched him approach. She told herself it was strictly because of the events that were going on but she wasn't sure whether she was just lying to herself because it helped. But the truth was he was an amazing man—especially in the kindness that he was showing her.

"Are you ready?"His gaze held hers with the care and strength of someone who could be counted on and leaned on.

She nodded; he reached for her bag and he beat her to it.

"Then let's go. The sooner we get going, the quicker you can see your dad."

"Don't worry about locking up. I'll take care of all that. You go," Jessica said.

She put her arms around Jessica. "Thank you for all you're doing."

Jessica frowned. "You don't owe me anything. That's what friends are for. Now go—and remember, your dad's going to be okay. So enjoy the ride." She winked."Got a ride with a handsome cowboy. And a helpful one at that. You can't beat that."

CHAPTER EIGHT

Moments later, she and Cam were traveling down the road. Cam wanted so much to make her feel better, he smiled at her, trying to encourage her.

"Can I get you a drink or anything before we get out of town?"

She had her hands cupped in her lap and she sat very stiff. If she stayed like that the whole trip, she was going to be in a knot of mangled tension by the time they got where they were going and would need a massage.

"I'm fine, really. I'm sure I'll need to stop at some point, just not now."

He smiled this time. "Sounds like a plan."

"So your ranch in Texas, tell me about it," she said after a few moments.

They were on the bridge heading out of Windswept Bay and going toward the mainland. They were surrounded by the sparkly blue water as the sun began to set dappling golden flecks onto the water.

"You love it there, don't you?" she continued.

"I do. It's beautiful in a different way than here. You know what I mean, being Texan yourself. I've got good neighbors and Sweet River, the town I live in, is not too big and the people are really nice—it's perfect. Grant—Cali's husband—he has a ranch next door. It'll be a great place for me to raise kids one day."

"Sounds like the town of Ransom Springs, Texas, where I'm from. There must have been a thing for water back when they named them." She smiled. "Ransom Springs is a nice size. I love my hometown, actually." She laughed softly and it was good to hear it. "But I came to Windswept Bay to get away. As I told you that day I came to the stable and practically told you my life story." She still couldn't believe she'd told him about Dave right after meeting him.

"So do you think you'll go back home?"

"Yesterday, I would have said no. Today, I'm not sure. I was trying to stand on my own, away from my overprotective dad and my brothers as much as to get away from the breakup fiasco. I grew tired of them trying to tell me how to live my life. They did it out of love but it just kind of drove me crazy. But now my dad…"Her words faded out and she looked out the window.

He heard the tears in her voice and glimpsed them in her eyes before she turned away. He didn't like to see her hurting. There was something deep going on here, he sensed it.

In the short time he had known her, Cam got the feeling Lana was one to cry easily and she didn't like anyone knowing she did. There was a softness to Lana that she tried to hide.

"You have to spread your wings at some point." He hoped it helped her feel better. Right now, with her dad so sick, he was unsure how to help her. "You have to find your own way and sometimes that means getting away. I did it."

"Really? You left to get away?"

"A little. I wanted to make it on my own. I'm geared that way. But there was no drama about me moving away, though. My family always knew I would go to Texas. Owning a ranch there with horses and cattle had always been my dream so I went looking for a job there as soon as I was old enough."

Her shoulders drooped and her eyes were troubled. He wanted to reach over and give her a hug.

"I didn't tell you how upset my dad was, is over my leaving. He's really obstinate, he doesn't understand."

"Why is that? Was he trying to hold you back? Did he not think you could make it?"He was watching the road and heard her sigh. He glanced at her and she grimaced.

"Maybe. But mostly I think he just wants me near him. But the pressure of my family always trying to tell me what to do gets old."

"Sounds like you had good reasons for leaving. You can't second-guess yourself."

"Yeah," she said, not sounding convinced. "Maybe. But now this…"

Cam couldn't help himself; he reached out and placed a hand on her forearm. "It's going to be okay, Lana. You need to give yourself some grace and some space and stop being so hard on yourself. I'm telling you, your dad will understand eventually. You're his baby girl and I'm pretty sure when you turn those pretty eyes of yours on him, there is not one thing that he wouldn't do to bring a smile to your face."

Her eyes widened a little bit and dug into his heartstrings all the more.

"You do have a way with words, Cam Sinclair."

He grinned. "I always try to be of help."

She laughed, a lighter laugh this time, and a band squeezed around his heart.

"You brighten my day. Made me think of my dad. He does like to make me smile. Always says it's like a ray of sunshine."

"That's a perfect description," he said, before he

caught himself.

But it was true. When she turned the full wattage on in that smile, it could very possibly melt him into a puddle. She probably didn't even know how powerful that smile of hers could be.

And maybe it was just the effect it had on him…

They drove for several miles without saying much. Lana wasn't sure whether Cam was deep in thought or just trying to give her some space, but the silence wasn't good for her mind. She kept thinking of her dad, lying in his hospital bed, alive, but she knew him and he was probably thinking about mortality right now. Thinking about how he could have died. And he was probably wondering how long he had to live.

She was.

Those thoughts were not soothing or helpful and they just made her want to scream. She needed to be there with him. To comfort him. To talk to him.

When she managed not to think about her dad, her thoughts shifted to the cowboy driving the truck beside her. Cam made her feel nervous, not get-on-an-airplane-sick kind of nervous but a jittery, nice kind of nervous. But every time he turned those penetrating blue eyes on her, she felt weak in the knees. Then she would reprimand herself for losing focus and go back to thinking about her dad. It was an odd merry-go-round of thoughts.

"So, I can't stand not talking. It's driving me batty, thinking about my dad and everything. So, tell me what's your favorite thing about the ranch…horses—are you a cutting horse man or is it the cattle you like? Or just like having the land?"

That toe-tingling smile came instantly to his lips. Her knees went weak. And there were butterflies, lots of butterflies. He did have an effect on her like none other ever had…even Dave.

"All of the above. I am a complete rancher cowboy. I love being on the land. I love taking my horse out on an early morning ride and seeing the sunrise over the horizon as I ride across the ranch. I love seeing my cattle taken care of. I like watching the mamas and then seeing the babies born, and the colts."

"I know you started riding at Bess's place but how did it all start, this infatuation?"

"Do you like old Westerns?"

"Very much."

"Me too. When I was a kid, I watched old movies with my grandpa. You know, John Wayne in *The Cowboys* was our favorite. When he had to hire on all those school boys because the men were all gone, I remember I was little bitty watching that movie but I wanted to be one of those little boys he chose to go on that cattle drive."

She laughed, visualizing him as a serious little boy watching that movie.

"I wanted to be that rough, tough cowboy like him. It never wore off."

Lana chuckled. "So are you a rough, tough cowboy?"

He laughed now. "I get the job done."

She liked watching him speak about the ranch. His face grew animated and he spoke with his hands when he could. And when he really meant something, his brows dipped in the center and his eyes sparked with life. It was enough to make a girl...*fall in love?*

The thought startled her. Blindsided her was more like it.

She hardly knew the man. She wasn't falling in love. She'd been there, done that. But he did have an effect on her and there was absolutely no sense denying that the man had a way.

"So you liked those movies set back in the Old West. Do you think that you would have rather lived back then, in those days?" She was really interested. She knew cowboys who did wish they'd been born back in the 1800s,deep in cowboy time. Not her.

"I know you expect me to say yes but the answer is no. I enjoy the conveniences of life. I enjoy the ability to see more country. Back then, it was really hard to see more country because it took so long to get there on horseback. I don't relish the idea of fighting Indians and I like hot showers a lot." He laughed. "I'm not a wimp but I like to go to bed clean, without having had to bathe in a stream. I like cattle drives that last no more than maybe two nights. Does all that surprise you?"

"A little. You seem so determined to get to Texas I guess I expected you to want to live back in the cowboy days. But I'm with you. I might be a cowgirl today but I like conveniences also. We have a lot in common."

"Yes we do," he drawled.

"My dad will like you. My brothers too. They are the same way, except my brother Vance. I think he would be a throwback. Before he hit the rodeo circuit hard, he took the winter and actually went north to work on a ranch in Montana. It was almost like living back in the 1800s because he was on a vast ranch in a tiny shack watching over a portion of the ranch through the winter."

"Yeah, that's rough. I have friends who have ranches up there and I've visited. Gorgeous in a different way from Texas, but beautiful. If he chose to go in the winter, he was looking for some hardship."He chuckled and shook his head.

"Yes, he was looking for a challenge. That's Vance. It's why he's chasing the NFR every year. Him and a bronc fighting it out in the arena suits him."

"It sounds like it."

The miles seemed to speed by as they opened up about their love of the ranch life. Lana had been trying to deny that she missed it but she did. In many ways, at least. Others, not so much.

CHAPTER NINE

They were traveling on the stretch of Florida that really had no view, just trees on both sides of the highway. Normally, a boring and endless stretch. Thankfully they'd been talking and it didn't seem so boring and endless with Cam at the wheel.

"Okay, is it time for a pit stop?" Cam asked.

"Yes, you read my mind. I could use a stretch of my legs and the ladies' room would be awesome. How did you know?"

"I was raised with four sisters."

"Oh yes. And I was raised with five brothers. They

can drive for hours and hours without stopping."

He chuckled. "Well, I'll take better care of you."

He took the exit and they pulled into the large, nice-looking truck stop area with a grassy section. He pulled the truck and trailer up to a gas pump. They walked to the back of the trailer to check on the horses. She peered through the rails and was happy to see that the mom and her baby were fine.

"Hey, little fella." She rubbed his neck when he moved to stand beside her. "You're a born traveler." The colt bucked his head back and then dropped his chin, as if to agree with her. She laughed. "Okay, I need to head inside. But I'll be back."

The colt whinnied and clawed his hoof on the wooden floor of the trailer. The mom looked on with pride.

Cam looked at the sky. "We might get into some bad weather. You go ahead. I'm going to fill up with gas and check the reports and then I'll be in."

"It is looking dark up there." Lana cringed. "I know you'd planned on leaving in the morning. You probably already knew there was going to be bad weather when you said you would carry me. I hope I haven't caused a problem."

"I've driven through bad weather before with horses and a trailer so I can do this. I didn't see any tornado warnings. You go ahead inside and it will be fine."

She still couldn't help but worry. He was a capable driver and she trusted him. She'd driven through her share of storms with livestock so she knew that it wasn't an uncommon thing to do. But she felt responsible.

A few minutes later, after she had been to the ladies' room and grabbed a cup of coffee and a bag of chocolate to share on the road, she headed back outside.

She was crossing the parking lot when she saw an older man and an older lady getting into their car sitting in the handicap zone. The lady seemed to be having a little bit of trouble as the man gently helped ease her down into the passenger seat.

Lana paused. "Do you need any help?"

The man smiled at her. "We're fine but thank you

for asking. My wife just has a bad back but she can do it."

The lady smiled at her and managed in that moment to sit. "Yes, I fell the other day and I messed my back up. I'll be fine soon. But getting in and out of the car is a hard thing to do right now. Thank you for offering to help. Are those your horses? We saw you get out of the truck as we were getting gas."

"No, ma'am, they're my friend's. He's taking them home to his ranch. In Texas."

"We're headed just across the border in Texas. It's a long drive."

"And bad weather is coming so y'all need to be safe."

"We'll be fine."

"Okay, take care." Lana moved toward the truck and trailer and watched the car pull out onto the road and then turn to get on the highway.

She hoped they got to their hotel soon and got out of the weather that was coming.

She smiled when she saw Cam come out of the store behind her. He'd come in while she'd been at the counter paying for her snacks. He carried his own cup of coffee.

He smiled at her and she had to admit that he brightened up her day.

Cam had been at the counter paying and saw through the window as Lana had talked with the older couple. He felt protective over her. He wasn't going to tell her that but he could see why her brothers and her dad wanted to protect her. Despite the fact that she was very much an independent woman, she was still a woman. Not that she was helpless; he had a feeling that if she got mad, she was probably a firecracker. Still, that wouldn't stop her family from trying to protect her and it wouldn't stop him from trying to protect her. She was a good person, it was easy to see.

He watched her hair swinging in motion with the gentle sway of her hips. He had thought the attraction he felt toward her would ease up. After all, she didn't want to move back to Texas and there was no use being attracted to someone who didn't want to live where he did. But it was a losing battle because there was definitely a strong and growing attraction.

She reached the truck and turned to lean against it.

"I would have gotten you some coffee if you'd asked," she said. "I should have asked you, though. I did get us a snack." She held up a good-sized bag of chocolate-covered peanuts.

"Now that looks like something I could do some damage to."

She grinned. "Me too. I don't know why travel always makes me want to snack on something."

"I'm not going to complain."

"You're my kind of man." She reached for the bag and suddenly her head came up. "I mean, I'm glad you like chocolate."

He chuckled, enjoying the rose tinge she'd turned.

"This will last till supper," she added.

He let her remark slide, feeling she wouldn't want him to tease her about being her kind of man. But he liked the idea.

"We'll stop for dinner a little farther down the road. If that's okay."

"I agree."

Within minutes, they were back on the road. She ripped open the container of peanuts, reached in, took out one small piece and held the bag out to him. "Grab a handful—they're delicious."

"Don't mind if I do." He held his hand out and she poured a good portion into his palm. He immediately popped a few into his mouth. "Not bad. Not bad at all."

She laughed. "You know you love them."

"Okay, I love them." He smiled and held his hand out for more.

They ate their way down the highway, enjoying the ease that had settled between them. In the distance, the storm clouds grew darker. He knew it wouldn't be long before they were right in the middle of it.

"What made you want to be a teacher?" he asked.

"I like kids and want to be involved in educating them. And, there is a personal reason, too, because I like the idea of having summers off with my own children eventually. Since my mom died when I was born, I didn't have a mother growing up. I want to be able to be home with my kids as much as possible."

Cam officially joined the Lana Presley fan club in that moment. "I like your way of thinking. I'm sorry you lost your mother. I know that was hard on you. I don't know what I'd do if I hadn't had my mom."

"As a little girl, I would pretend that I was like other little girls and that my mother was alive. She was like my invisible friend."

Cam got a lump in his throat at her words. It was incredibly sad to imagine her with her invisible friend. "People cope in many different ways—that's a sad way for you to cope." He reached over and squeezed her shoulder, wanting to comfort her in some way. "I hope you have a house full of kids for yourself and you get to experience being a mom."

"Thank you," she said, softly meeting his gaze before he focused on the road. "I hope for a house full too." She laughed as his gaze swung back to her. Her eyes twinkled."I hope I have a few girls with a few boys."

He laughed. "Well, even if you have five sons and one daughter, your daughter will have you."

"God willing, yes, she will. And she will also have

her brothers. My brothers were great—overprotective, it's true—but I'd give anything for any one of them. They're wonderful."

"They obviously care for you. Which I have to admit is easy to do. You make me want to protect you…so I understand where they're coming from." He glanced back at her, unsure how she would take the truth.

"You've quickly become a great friend to me, Cam. I've told you so much about my life and I'm not usually so chatty about my personal business. But I've told you."

"I'm glad you felt comfortable talking to me. I hope you're telling me this because you trust me. I *can* be trusted. I'm sure after what you just went through, trust is something you have trouble with."

"Oh wise one. You're right. I struggle with trust issues. So much so that I haven't started dating. Which is odd since I had no trouble telling Jessica she needed to get back into the dating pool when Levi came along. I had no problem telling her to trust."

"Hey, we are talking about Levi. What's not to

trust about my brother? If he can't be trusted, no one can."

"True. But when you've been hurt, it's hard to get your heart to believe it. But you trust me?"Her lips curved upward. "We aren't talking about the dating pool but about a friend helping a friend out by giving her a ride home."

"You're talking about that. I'm talking about that too, but I'm also hoping for the possibility of a date."

"Oh."She stared at him in disbelief. "Really…"

The heavens opened up in that moment, making continuing the conversation difficult for now. But there was no way he was abandoning it. Storm or no storm, he was going to pursue getting Lana to agree to give him a chance at a date.

Lightning lit up the sky and almost instantly thunder cracked, shaking the truck.

Lana knew they were in for a ride but Cam had both hands on the wheel and had slowed his speed. It was easy to tell that he had driven through all kinds of weather pulling a trailer.

"This is getting rough. Check your weather app and see if there are any tornadoes in the area."

She pulled her phone out and pulled up the Weather Channel. Instantly, she saw the alerts. "Oh yes, definitely under tornado watch. There are several warnings out there right now." A chill of worry filled her. She sat up and scanned the dark sky. Not that she could see anything.

"I was afraid of that. But I think we'll be okay. We'll take the next exit and stop for supper and try to watch a news report."

"That sounds good."

A few minutes later, they pulled onto an exit and headed toward a diner. Even from outside, they could see the glow of the TV in the bar area. "That should be good and we can watch the trailer from there with all the windows like that. It's not exactly where I was hoping to take you for dinner."

His words took her attention off the storm for a moment. *The man wanted to take her somewhere nice for dinner.* The thought was nice. And despite the fact that she hadn't been on a date in a year because she wasn't ready to trust anyone, the man seemed to understand what was going on in her head. *Did he know she was thinking a nice dinner with him was suddenly very appealing?*

He parked the truck and trailer. After he turned off the engine, he reached behind the seat into the floorboard of the truck and pulled out an umbrella. He handed it to her. Their fingers brushed and a shiver of awareness shot up her arm.

"I'm not sure it will protect you too much with the way the wind is whipping but it's worth a try."He pulled out a plastic hat cover and fit it on his hat to protect his hat from the rain. And then he grabbed a rain jacket and shrugged into it. "You go ahead inside. I need to check on the horses. Do you need a jacket? I'll give you this one if you do."

"I'll be fine. I have a windbreaker that will protect me." She reached into her bag. "You sure you don't need me?"

"No, I'm fine. I'm glad you have those boots on. Your feet are going to get swamped in that water. I should have let you out at the door."

"I won't melt. I've done this before," she said. "But it's nice that you are thinking about that. See you in a minute."She jumped out of the truck and headed inside.

She paused inside the doorway to wait for Cam. She peeled off the now soaked jacket. Cam was going to be soaked; she could see him through the darkness as he checked on the horses and then jogged across the flooding parking lot.

She pushed the door open for him. He took his hat off. "We stopped at a really good time." He pulled off his jacket and hung it on a rack next to the door.

They entered through the secondary door into the diner.

The hostess approached them. "You folks stopping by to get out of the storm?"

"Yes. It's awful out there," Lana said. "Are there tornadoes around?"

The waitress nodded. "Yes. But this is the safest place to be right now. Do you want a seat in the bar area so you can watch the news?"

"That would be good," Cam said.

The woman led them to the last table in the bar.

She scanned the diner."I'm glad we're here but I feel bad for everyone caught out in this storm who can't get to safety. I hope that older couple seeks shelter somewhere."

"I do too." He reached for a menu and scanned it. She did the same. "I'm thinking those fajitas are in my future."

She closed the menu. "All I can say is we are on the same wavelength because I see those in my future too."

He grinned. "Then fajitas for two coming up."

The waitress came back and he gave her their order. She'd just walked away when thunder rattled the diner's windows and instantly the lights went out.

CHAPTER TEN

"Just what I hoped we'd miss." Lana groaned the instant the lights went out.

Cam reached across the table and covered Lana's hand with his. "It's going to be okay," he said, wanting to reassure her. He suspected the storm was adding more stress to her already full plate. "I'll get you to your dad, so don't let this weather put more stress on you."

"Thanks, but it's really bad out there. I know my dad is doing okay but this is going to slow us down."

Everyone in the diner had started talking louder,

and some were up, moving around to look out the windows. He was going to have to do something with the horses but his options were limited at the moment. This wasn't the sturdiest diner he'd ever seen either. If a tornado set down on them, they didn't have much more shelter than the horses did in their trailer.

"I'll get you there, I promise," he said, trying again to reassure her.

"Thanks. But we could be in a pickle."Lana turned her hand over beneath his and held his hand.

His pulse quickened at her action.

One thing he'd learned about Lana was she didn't really sugarcoat anything. "Yes, we could be. But I'm thinking positive. I'm going to go out and look around, see if I can hear or see anything when the next flash of lightning strikes. Stay here, away from the windows, and get ready to get under this table if you need to." He could make out her expression in the darkness. Her hand tightened on his.

"Be careful. I can come too—"

"No, you stay here. I mean it, Lana," he warned when she moved to get up.

"Fine. I'll wait, but if you don't come back in soon, I'll be coming out there."

He stood and moved to her side of the table and then leaned down, bringing his face close to hers in the darkness. The soft scent of her shampoo had him wanting to lean closer."Stay put. I'll be back. I don't want your brothers and your dad coming after me." And then, unable to stop himself, he kissed her. He'd been wanting to kiss her again ever since that time in the barn and now, he did it.

She gasped as his lips captured hers; then her hand came to cup his jaw and she leaned into the kiss. His adrenaline spiked and his breath caught in his chest.

"I'll be back," he murmured and then he left her and strode to the door. Lightning flashed and thunder exploded just as he walked into the outer entrance to grab his raincoat. At least he thought it was the weather going crazy around him…it could have been the effects of that kiss because there was definitely fireworks and rockets exploding for him right now.

It was all Lana could do not to go with Cam. She jumped from her seat, her heart pounding like the thunder outside from the kiss they'd shared. Compounded with that, worry for him knotted her insides.

This storm had turned nasty.

The weather report on the television was no longer an option, so she pulled it up on her phone and was glad to see she could still pull up a report on it. There were flood watch reports all over the place. It had gone from bad to dangerous in zero to sixty seconds. Lightning lit the sky again and she saw Cam get inside the truck. Then he started it up. If she was right, he was moving the trailer to the side of the diner that would give the animals a little relief from the rain. His trailer was nice in that it was a hauler and had sides and a roof versus an all railed open trailer, thus giving the horses protection from most of the rain. He'd closed the window earlier before coming into the diner; still, the wind buffeted the sides and she had a feeling the horses were getting nervous. He did as she thought and pulled the trailer around to the back. A few moments later, she glimpsed him jogging through the rain toward the door.

Relief washed over her as he entered the diner once more. He was safe—or as safe as they could be given the situation. Unable to stop herself, she rushed forward and wrapped her arms around him.

"Hey, you're going to get wet." He half laughed but held her against him.

"I'm glad you're safe." Then, feeling self-conscious, she pulled out of his arms. Her shirt was wet now but she didn't care. She was just so happy he was okay.

The waitress was passing out candles and brought one to their table."Would you like some coffee, cowboy? We still have some that's warm since the lights haven't been off long."

"That would be great." Cam peeled off his jacket and laid it in the empty booth next to theirs. "Do y'all have an emergency generator?"

"Sorry. It's not working. But our cook called the police—his brother is one of the deputies—and he told him the danger is almost over. I'll bring the coffee. Might as well sit down there and snuggle."

Lana had to admit it sounded like a good idea. "I

think it's going to blow over soon, as long as a twister doesn't develop in the next few minutes."

"Let's hope you're right." He smiled in the candlelight. "Until then, we'll just wait it out. At least I have great company."

She smiled and slid into the booth, making room for him as the waitress brought his coffee and a cup for Lana, too, and set it on the table.

"Enjoy. Maybe that'll help take the wet chill off. You got pretty wet out there," she said.

"I'll be fine. I've been soaked before. Thanks for the coffee. Let me know if I can help out with anything," Cam offered.

"Thank you, but we're just going to have to sit it out. Looks like we have a pretty calm crowd." She headed off to take care of the other customers waiting out the storm.

"So now we wait."Cam picked up the cup. Lightning struck outside and lit up the sky once more. "Looks like we might as well enjoy the show."

And what a show it was. The lightning flashed and the thunder rolled. Though they stayed away from the big windows, they still had a great view of nature in all its glory—or fury—as they talked and watched the night.

Two hours later, the storm eased up.

"We better take our shot," Cam said. They jogged through the rain and climbed back into the truck.

"That's crazy!"She laughed, breathless as she pulled the door closed behind her.

"Tell me about it. Okay, let's get you home to your dad. Maybe you should try to sleep so you won't be worn-out when we get there."

"I won't be able to, I don't think. Not knowing you're not going to get any rest."

"I do this all the time. I'll be fine."

"We'll see." She watched the dark road. "Not many people out now," she said, hoping to change the subject.

"Most people found shelter and aren't driving around yet. But we have an important place to get to." He shot her an easy smile that was kind and made her like him all the more.

"That makes sense. If I wasn't trying to get home, I wouldn't be on the road either."

Farther along, they passed several cars sitting on the side of the road and in different segments of the next ten miles. "They got caught in the storm. I bet that was scary, sitting it out in their cars." She felt for them. It had been scary enough in the diner.

"Looks like that's what happened."

Suddenly, she spotted a car she recognized. "Cam, that was that older couple I spoke to earlier this afternoon. He was standing outside the car."

"I think he was trying to fix a flat." Cam began to slow the truck as he spoke.

"Are you going to help them?"

"Yes. I hope you don't mind?"

"Oh no, I'm glad. I want to help them."

"Good. I will get you to your dad."

She smiled at him. "I know you will. But passing them up on the side of the road would haunt me forever, so thank you."

"I'll take that emergency cross-over up there. If it

looks like we can get the trailer through it. That depends on what the rain did to it…"He slowed and then pulled to the shoulder as he checked out the ground between the highway lanes. "Looks good. I think we can make it."

She was relieved when they made it back onto the highway going the opposite way and within a few more minutes after going back through another emergency crossroad, they pulled up behind the car. The poor man looked so relieved when they pulled up behind him. When she and Cam hopped from the truck and walked toward him, recognition came instantly to his startled expression.

"I know you."

She smiled. "Yes, we crossed paths earlier this afternoon. We saw you and thought you might need some help."

His eyes widened in relief. "I would be so grateful."

"Did y'all have to go through the storm here on the side of the road?" Cam asked.

"Yes, we missed the exit. It was a scary mistake.

My wife is still upset over it."

"We'll take care of this for you."

She moved to the window on the passenger side of the car; the lady looked up and instantly looked excited. She rolled her window down.

"Hello there. You're that nice young woman from the store this afternoon."

"I am. My name is Lana Presley and my friend is Cam Sinclair. He's going to change your tire and I'm going to help him. I just wanted to say hello."

"I'm Clara and my husband is Jim. It is so wonderful of you to stop and help. This has been a terrifying night, I don't mind telling you."

"I can only imagine how terrifying it must have been sitting here in the car. We'll get you back on the road so hopefully you two can find a room for the night and relax before you get back on the road tomorrow."

Clara sighed and dabbed at tears that suddenly filled her eyes and glistened in the interior light of the car. Lana was so thankful that she and Cam had spotted them on the side of the road.

"Relax, okay? I better go help Cam. I'll talk to you in a minute."

She hurried back to Cam and Jim. He looked worn-out and she wasn't sure that he was in the best of health himself. This couple needed to get wherever they were going, that was completely evident. "I'll help Cam get this tire on. Why don't you go sit in the car with Clara? She seems worried."

He started to argue but Cam stopped him. "Really, Jim, it's okay. We can do this and you need to get out of this rain because your wife is going to need you to get her to safety somewhere. If you stand out here and exhaust yourself anymore, you might not be able to take care of her like you need to."

That got him; Lana saw it in his eyes. "Okay. You're probably right."

"Your wife is your priority, so don't feel bad. We'll have you on the road in a few minutes."

Lana could have hugged Cam in that moment. The one way to get this older man to accommodate them was to talk about him providing shelter for his wife. And protection. It hopefully gave him the excuse to do as they asked because he literally looked as if he needed to see a doctor himself.

"Thank you. I have been ill and this is really hard. We shouldn't have made this trip. But my wife's brother passed away and I could not let her miss his funeral, so we made this trip and coming off illness myself, it's been tough."

Cam patted his shoulder. "I'm sure sorry, sir, for your loss. But that's why you need to go get in the car. It's okay. We've got this."

It was all Lana could do not to throw her arms around Cam Sinclair and hug the stuffing out of him in that moment. *What a hero…he was almost too perfect to believe.* She watched Jim nod and then go and get inside the car. She looked at Cam. Water dripped off his hat and rolled down his face. She knew that she looked the same but didn't care.

She smiled through the water and then did what she felt like doing. She took two steps, put her arms around his waist and hugged him tightly."Thank you. You knew exactly how to speak to him in order to get him to do what was needed."

Cam hugged her close, melding their soaked bodies together. "You do know you're soaked, don't you?"

She laughed. "Yes, and you are too but I don't care in the least. You're an amazing man, Cam." She couldn't have cared less about the wind and the rain; all she could think about were his arms wrapped around her and the feel of his heart beating against hers. There was no other place on earth in that moment she would rather be.

"I'm glad you saw them and if I can get thanks like this, then I'll start being helpful to everyone on the side of the road between here and Texas."

She chuckled and stepped out of his arms. "Don't push your luck, cowboy," she said, though to be honest, that sounded like a great plan to her. "We better get to work and get this sweet couple on the road again."

He tipped his wet hat. "Yes, ma'am," he drawled. His eyes glittered merrily in the light from the truck's low beams.

Lana stood the tire up that Jim had managed to get

out of the trunk before they'd gotten there. She rolled it over and watched as Cam got the jack under the car and jacked it up. He made quick work of getting the lug nuts off the wheel. Within moments, he had the flat tire on the ground and took the spare from her. She felt fairly useless but had enjoyed watching him work. Yes, she was very capable of changing a tire by herself— her dad and brothers had made sure of it. Besides that, any cowgirl worth her salt who hauled horses around better know how to take care of herself on the road. But she hadn't had to break out her skills on this go-round. And the view had been fantastic.

Rain dripped from both their faces and they were soaked to the bone but smiling. She couldn't help admiring the man who diligently worked to make the night better for this older couple.

After he removed the jack, he stood and laughed. "We are a pair."

She laughed. "A soaked pair. But you did good, cowboy. Real good."

"You're not so bad yourself. How are you holding up?"

"I'm doing great," she said through the wind. "Like I said earlier, I'm not made of sugar so I don't melt."

"I have to differ with you on that. I think you're plenty sweet. There aren't many women who would stand out here and do this. And you haven't complained once. I'm really surprised you haven't melted."

She felt his words in the center of her heart. Which was ridiculous. The man was teasing her. But still, she felt them.

Jim and Clara argued with them about paying them something but finally relented and went on their way. But they'd made them promise that if they were ever near their address that they'd come by for dinner.

After watching their headlights disappear, they walked back to the truck. No reason to get in a hurry considering they could not get any more soaked than they already were.

Cam placed his arm lightly over her shoulders as they walked and Lana leaned her head onto his shoulder. She had bonded with this man; there was no denying it. They had been on the road for less than nine hours and yet it felt as though they had been together for a while. A good while.

She really liked him—liked his kindness, his goodness—and there was no denying it. He opened her door and waited for her to get inside. "Your poor seats. They're going to be ruined."

"Not a problem. This is a working ranch truck. It's no big deal."

There was nothing she could do about his seats so she climbed inside, cringing as she sank onto the leather. "They will never look the same again."

Cam chuckled. "Stop it. They're seats." He closed her door and then strode around the front of the truck, the rain shining in the headlights on him. When he climbed inside and slammed the door, he immediately turned up the heat. "As soon as I see a place with an overhang that I can park this rig under, I'll stop and let you change in the sleeping quarters of the trailer. Then I'll do the same. I'll dry the seat some while you're changing. I'm sorry it's taking us so long."

"My dad would have been upset if we hadn't

stopped because of him."

"Well, you're very gracious. And I know you're worried about your dad. But I have to tell you that I like how you put your own needs aside and wanted to stop and help them."

Lana took a deep breath. "I'm praying my dad is still holding stable like my brother last texted me. I texted him while you were out in the storm and told him what was going on and he told me everything was still good. But, like I said, my dad would have wanted us to stop and help them."

"I'm looking forward to meeting your dad." He pulled back out onto the highway and got the truck up to speed. "Like I said, when I find a place to park this rig I'll dry the seat while you're changing into dry clothes. Then I'll change."

"Sounds good. And just so you know, you'll be on my dad's good side for what you've done so far." She chuckled.

"Not if you catch a cold because you're soaked."

At the next exit, he pulled under the protective awning of a gas station and while he filled the truck up with gas, she changed inside the small quarters at the front of the horse trailer. It was a really nice setup. Very similar to the one her family owned. There was a double bed on the upper level and a small couch used for seating in the small kitchenette area. It was decorated beautifully, with plenty of room to move around.

After she'd changed, she headed outside. He smiled at her and butterflies fluttered in her chest. Oh yes, it was definitely a moment of acknowledgment that this guy had her interest. Despite her bad relationship before, Cam was quickly overcoming any reservations she might've had.

"You look like you feel better," he said, filling the sudden awkward silence looming between them.

"I…do." Nerves rattled through her and he seemed nervous too.

He moved so she could see the passenger seat. "I put a towel on the seat for you. The leather was still damp."

"Thank you. Now, please, it's your turn to head in there and dry off." She needed him to head in there and give her a moment to get her head on straight. There were so many reasons she shouldn't be feeling this attraction. But right now all she wanted to do was kiss the man. He'd been so wonderful this entire trip.

"I think I'll do that." Instead of moving, he lifted his hand and ran the back of his fingers against her jaw. "I'll be right back."

And then he strode away. She didn't start breathing again until he disappeared inside the trailer.

CHAPTER ELEVEN

It was two in the afternoon when they finally rolled into the hospital parking lot.

Cam was not ready to say good-bye to Lana. He'd realized during the ride that he wanted to pursue a relationship with her. Wanted to get to know her better because he thought she was special. The way she'd wanted to help that couple on the road and had never complained though they'd gotten soaked had made an impression on him like none other.

He was tired and ready for a nap but he didn't want to leave. She'd freshened up on the last stop and though she looked tired, she was as pretty as a picture.

"I'm going to forever be grateful for you for doing

this," she told him again.

"You don't have to be grateful to me. I was glad to do it and I wouldn't have missed getting to know you better. That was a bonus."

She smiled. "I feel the same way."

"I'm going to park the truck in the back of the parking area and I'm going to get in the trailer apartment and catch a couple of hours sleep. You go see your dad and then I'll message you before I get back on the road. Maybe you can come down and see me off."

"I would like that. I also want you to come meet Dad before you go. He would be upset if you left without meeting him."

The doors of the hospital opened and five cowboys walked outside.

Cam saw the smile that came to Lana's face. There was no mistaking who they were by that look on her face but he would have known who they were even if she hadn't been smiling...the resemblance was striking.

"Oh boy, you're about to meet the Presley

brothers. They must've been waiting. We are kind of noticeable with this large horse trailer behind us."

He laughed. "I'd say so. And I'll say this again—I'm glad I got you here safe or my hide might have been toast."

She chuckled at that. "I hate to say this, but you might be right. Though I have a good feeling you can handle yourself quite well."

He'd have said more but there was no time as the brothers arrived…and surrounded him.

Lana couldn't believe how great it felt to see her brothers. The last time she'd seen them, it had been strained. They had all been together at Christmas but they had been unhappy that she'd moved away from the ranch and family. But this was different. Relief swamped her. Relief that she was here with them…her family—Shane, Drake, Cooper, Vance, and Brice—and she needed hugs from them so bad.

They weren't smiling—her stomach dropped. "Is Dad okay?"She had the sudden horrifying thought that they'd told her Dad was okay just to get her home safely when he was really *not* okay.

"Hold on," Cooper and Drake said at the same time.

"He's fine," Drake added, quickly. "I told you he was fine. He's waiting to see you."

"You can breathe now," Shane added and moved to hug her. "We're glad you're home. We all came to greet you because we've missed you."

Brice tugged her away from Shane. "Yeah, bug. We did miss you but we also wanted to meet the man who brought you home to us."

She hugged him back, suddenly wanting to cry as all her brothers hugged her."Y'all are going to make me cry." Then she caught a glimpse of Cam. He was watching them with a smile. She broke away and moved toward him.

"This is Cam. He found out I was going to drive and insisted on driving me since I was upset."

Cooper squinted and held out his hand. "You insisted and she did what you wanted? How does that work? I'm Cooper. And this is Drake, Shane, Vance, and Brice."

Cam shook all their hands as each one needled him about her agreeing with what he wanted.

"Okay, guys. Stop teasing. Cam is worn-out and is going to go catch some shut-eye before he heads on to his ranch and I'm going to go see Dad."

"We'll take you up," Drake offered. "Cam, thank you. I know you need to go rest but before you leave, come see Dad if you have time. You're more than welcome to drive out to the ranch and rest."

"Thanks but I'll stay here. I'm only going to nap," Cam said. Stepping up, his gaze slid to Lana. "I'll see you in a couple of hours."

She nodded. "Good. I'll be right here." *Where she belonged.* But that didn't stop the tug at her heart knowing he would be leaving soon.

Cam watched Lana head into the hospital with her brothers. He was glad he'd brought her home. He climbed back into his truck and drove around to the back of the parking lot and parked the truck. It had been a long drive and fairly stressful with the weather but still he thought he might have trouble sleeping. He could tell her brothers cared about her. He had a feeling they'd given her a hard time about the jerk of a boyfriend she'd had because they'd known he wasn't worth his salt. Still, he understood her side of the trouble between them. It would have to be hard to be the only female up against a herd of brothers and a dad who all cared for her. She'd been smothered. He'd heard his sisters complain about him and his brothers smothering them and there had been four of them. His sisters bonded together to set their Sinclair brothers straight. He smiled, thinking of all the times there had been battles at home, growing up, between the brothers and the sisters. Poor Lana had been one against six.

But there was love here and that was clearly evident. *But would she want to come back here? She'd said she loved Windswept Bay...*

Lana entered her dad's room. Her brothers waited

outside to give her time alone with him. Her heart stuttered as she saw big, strong Marcus Presley wearing a green hospital gown and all kinds of IVs and monitors hooked up to him. She stopped short and her breath caught in her throat, aching with the sudden tears that threatened to overflow.

As if sensing her presence, he opened his eyes. "Baby girl," he said, her nickname.

She bit back the tears, forced them down and pulled herself forward. "Dad, this is a little extreme, don't you think? I'd have come home for a visit if you'd just asked. You did not have to have a heart attack."

He chuckled and held out his hand. "Whatever it takes to get you home."

She crossed to his bed and leaned over the bed, into his open arms. Unable to stop the tears, she felt his hospital gown dampen as she buried her face against his shoulder. "I'm so glad you're okay. You scared me."

His arms tightened around her and she felt him

kiss her head. "I love you, Lana. Don't you ever forget that."

Her heart ached and though she had held it together for miles across five states while getting here to him, the worry for him had been clamped around her heart. The storms and the weather had been great distractions from the stress that she felt but seeing her dad in this hospital bed, wearing a stupid hospital gown instead of his regular Western shirt and cowboy hat and jeans, killed her.

"Don't cry, baby girl." He patted her shoulder. "I'm sorry, so sorry. I should have understood why you wanted to leave. I should have supported you in your being upset about the breakup between you and that jerk instead of expecting you to just brush off the pain he'd put you through."

She pulled away and looked down at him. "It's okay, Dad. No need to talk about that now. All that matters is that you're alive and going to get better."

His gray eyes narrowed. "We'll talk about it later. But tell me about this fella who brought you home. Sounds like a good guy."

She smiled, thinking of Cam. "He is a really good guy."*The best of the best.*

Cam had been wrong. He'd set his alarm for two hours, lay down on the bunk in the sleeping quarters, and the next thing he knew, it was going off, letting him know it was time to get up.

He sat up, rubbed his face and then stood. It was time to see Lana again. He moved into the small bathroom to brush his teeth and wash his face. He stared at his stubble on his face and thought about shaving but decided he'd wait until he got home to do that. He wondered whether Lana liked a man with a beard or a smooth face. He'd never considered what a woman would prefer or not prefer until now. But truth was Lana had him thinking about a lot of things he'd never considered before.

Leaving her was going to be hard.

He checked on his horses and knew they'd be more than happy to get to the ranch but they were still doing fine. He wouldn't hang around long, though, because he needed to get them home. At least the horses' needs would give him a strong reason to get in the truck and drive away from Lana.

A few minutes later, he headed to Marcus Presley's room. He knocked on the slightly ajar door and waited until she pulled it open. "Cam, you're awake. Come in." Her smile was instant, sending his heart thundering and causing a feeling of longing to flow through him.

"Sure." He removed his hat as he stepped into the room.

"Dad, this is Cam Sinclair."

The man in the hospital bed looked sharply at him, assessing him. He looked about as comfortable in a green hospital gown as Cam would be and though he had a little gray hair at his temples, Marcus Presley, on any other week than the one he'd had a heart attack in, would probably look younger than his fifty-something years of age.

Today he looked a bit weak but the determination in his gray eyes told Cam that he'd be fighting his way back to health with every coming day.

Marcus held out his hand. "Excuse the IVs. They seem to think I need them. I want to thank you for bringing Lana home and getting her here safe through all the storms I heard y'all had to get through."

Cam shook his hand, and like he'd thought, Marcus's handshake was strong. "It was my privilege to do it. You have a great daughter. How are you feeling, sir?"

Marcus folded his hands."Glad to be alive. And happy to see Lana. Something like this makes you understand what's important in this world. I hear you have a ranch over near Madisonville. I've heard good things about your livestock."

"I think so." They talked about their ranches while Lana listened but didn't say much. He could tell she was just glad to listen to her dad talking. He decided on the drive between here and his ranch that he'd call his own dad and talk to him.

An hour later, Lana walked him out to the trailer.

"Thanks for talking to Dad and for putting up with my brothers."

Her brothers Drake and Vance had come back up

from the cafeteria before he'd left and he'd enjoyed talking to them. Her other brothers had gone back to the ranch to work.

"You have a great family. I like them."

"They are great. Obstinate but they mean well."

He slipped his arm over her shoulders as they neared his trailer. "They care about you. So tell me, are you going to be all right here?"

She smiled. "I'll be great."

"What about if you run into that ex-boyfriend?"

She laughed. "I'm pretty sure it's not going to bother me at all. Somewhere along the road here, I stopped caring at all."

He stopped walking and cocked his head to the side, studying her. "I'm glad to hear that. You're worth more than that."

"Thanks."

"Call me if you need me. And if you need a ride home, give me a call."

She chuckled. "Thank you, but I'm going to stay at least a week, maybe a little longer..." Her expression grew troubled.

"You're worrying again."

"Yes. I can't tell you how hard it was seeing him lying there. I just don't know if I can leave."

He kissed her forehead, couldn't stop himself. "You'll figure it out. I'm here if you need me."

"Thank you." She kissed his cheek. "For everything."

He wanted to talk more, to ask more, but now was not the time. He kissed her lips in a brief brush and then stepped back. If he'd let himself, he'd have kissed her forever. But now wasn't the time for that either. "I'll be talking to you. Take care of yourself and I'll be keeping your dad in my prayers."

"That means a lot."

And then, far too quickly, he was on the road again. Headed away from the first woman he'd ever had the desire to marry.

And he knew that was exactly what he felt for Lana. Somewhere between Windswept Bay and Ransom Springs, Texas, he'd fallen in love with Lana Presley.

CHAPTER TWELVE

Three hours later, Cam pulled into his ranch and as always, the feeling of home overcame him. He loved Windswept Bay and loved going home to visit and see his family but his heart was here in Texas on this ranch. He wanted more than anything to bring Lana here. To have her come see where he lived and what he'd built.

He dropped the horses off at the stables with one of the cowboys who worked for him and then he went to his house. Made of Austin rock and cedar, it had a rustic but inviting look to it. He wondered whether

Lana would like it. That had become the question of the day.

He rubbed his eyes as he entered the side entrance, stopped off in the kitchen to put on a pot of coffee and then he headed for the shower.

Unlike all the other times he'd come home, suddenly his house seemed lonesome. Too quiet. Too big. Too empty.

He was thirty-three years old and although he'd started hoping that the right woman would come into his life, he'd not been rushing it. He'd been content. That feeling did not describe what he was feeling right now.

He'd known Lana for a little less than a week and she felt right. She probably would think he was crazy but right now that was how he felt…crazy about her.

He finished his shower and dressed quickly. One thing he'd decided on the drive home was that he wasn't about to let this opportunity with Lana slip away.

He took the time to shave and then he went and lay down on the bed, knowing it was time to get more than a couple of hours of sleep. He'd been awake for fifteen hours, not counting the catnap he'd taken. Hopefully he would sleep because first thing in the morning, he was heading back to the hospital. He owed Lana a nice meal.

"Dad, I know you don't want that pudding but it's pudding you shall have."Lana glared at her dad. He was feeling better because he was being his obstinate, bull-headed self. He had given her the scare of her life with this heart attack and now he wanted to do things his way and not what the doctor was ordering.

"Lana, I'm not one of your first graders and I don't eat pudding."

"Then at least eat your chicken."

"That is rubber, not meat. I want a steak."

Men. She had sent all of her brothers back to work. There was a lot going on at the ranch this time of year and they had been alternating out duties but tomorrow was a big sell that had been in the works and they needed to be there to get ready. Her dad wanted to be there and that was part of the problem.

"Earlier, you were saying you had a new lease on life and you knew what was important."

His gaze narrowed, his handsome face going slack as he stared at her. "Honey, I do know what is important and it's not pudding or rubber chicken. It's you and your brothers and the ranch." His jaw tightened. "I'm ready to go home."

"I know that. But you have to do what you're told. Your diet has to change. And stop worrying about the ranch. The boys are handling it. You know that."

He loved everything about ranching and she knew his worry had nothing to do with thinking they couldn't handle it. He just wanted to be there.

His nurse came back into the room. She'd stepped out to give them some time to work on the meal troubles. She was a petite brunette named Karla. At maybe five foot tall and maybe a hundred pounds soaking wet, the woman was small but she was a firecracker.

Now, she put her hands on her hips. "Well, Mr. Presley, I see you still haven't eaten any of your meal."

Though she smiled, Lana heard the firmness in her voice. She was not happy about him not eating."I told you that you need to build your strength back and you have to change your diet. You had a heart attack, which means that you can't be eating steak and potatoes all the time anymore. And right now especially your diet needs to be bland. You must cut down on salt, red meat, and potatoes."

He glared at her. "Do I look like I've been eating a lot of potatoes?" He patted his flat stomach.

Lana couldn't help smiling. Her dad was in shape for a fifty-eight-year-old man. He rode horses and trained every day and still built fences on the ranch, right along with all his sons and ranch hands. He did not look like a man who was a candidate for a heart attack. All the more reason that they were startled that he had had a heart attack.

Karla's brow hitched. "It's very obvious you're in shape. But you like red meat and salt too much. Your cholesterol, sir, is off the charts. That cholesterol pill the doctor has prescribed will help but you have to change your diet. And that is just the way it is if you want to stay healthy."

Lana watched her dad and Karla glare at each other. *Was that a spark of interest she saw in her dad's eyes?* There weren't very many women who would stand up to his ill temper. He was used to getting his way when he was determined but it was obvious that Karla was used to getting her way too, despite being so small.

"And if you want to go home, then you have to eat."

Those were the magic words.

"Fine. Then push that cart back over here," he instructed Lana.

Holding back a grin, Lana pushed the cart back into place so the plate of food was in front of him. "Now you're on the right track," she said as he picked up the fork.

"I'm just doing this so I get to go home."

She smiled. "Whatever it takes is fine with me. Karla, you're going to have to excuse him. My dad is not used to sitting and as you can tell, it's getting tough for him to be stuck in this room."

"I can tell that. And I understand. But still, Marcus, you need to seriously change some things about your diet. Just a few changes can make a lot of difference. You're going to get out of here tomorrow but if you don't change you'll be back. And I know this is not where you want to be."

She smiled at him and Lana watched the two stare at each other. And then Karla blushed. Lana glanced back at her dad, who suddenly looked thoughtful.

"Well," Karla said. "I need to make rounds. I'll be back."

And then she left the room and to Lana's surprise, her dad ate.

Lana was suddenly thinking about her dad's social life. His dating life. As far as she knew, he didn't date much. And maybe it was time.

Just like it was time for her to get back to it too.

At her dad's insistence that he was fine at the hospital by himself, she went home that night to sleep. She showered before she crawled into bed and she didn't think that hot water had ever felt so good. Her bed felt like heaven and despite all that she had on her mind, she was asleep almost the instant her head hit the pillow.

The next morning, feeling more refreshed, she dressed and went downstairs. She had woken up with Cam on her mind. She wondered what he was doing. And whether he'd made it to his ranch okay. She had almost called him to check yesterday but then hadn't let herself.

"Morning."

Drake was getting coffee when she entered the kitchen. He wore chaps with his jeans, boots, and spurs. His long-sleeved shirt had a film of dust on it. He'd been working the horses in the round pen already. His hat was on the peg beside the back door."Good morning." He handed her the cup of coffee he'd just poured.

"Thanks." She took a barstool as he poured another cup for himself.

"So, Dad's getting to come home today. That's wonderful news." Drake leaned against the granite counter and took an easy drink of the hot coffee. "What do we need to do around here to get ready for him?"

She set her coffee down after she took a sip. "I think we just need to make sure there's food he can eat on his heart healthy diet and all of you need to encourage him to eat better. It wouldn't hurt all of you to eat less beef."

Drake nodded. "Gotcha. We can do that. Can you bring him home, or do you need one of us to come help? I can go or Coop. It's going to be busy around here today with the sale going on."

She knew all about it on the days they had a cattle sale. Buyers came from all over. "I can do it. If he knew one of you were leaving the sale to come cart him home, it would just add stress to him."

"Okay, then that's fine. But if you need me, I'll be there. It's really good to have you home. How long will you stay?"

"Thanks. I'll try to stay two weeks if possible."

"That sounds good. Of course, you know we'd love for you to come home for good."

"I'm thinking about it. But I don't know if that's the best thing. I've started a new life in Windswept Bay and I really love it there."

"It would put you closer to Cam."

"Cam just gave me a ride home."

"Oh really, is that all you think he did? Because the way he was looking at you said a different story."

She did not want to discuss her love life with her brother. "Drake, does Dad date?" she asked to change the subject.

"Okay, so I'll get out of your love life. I know a subject change when I hear it. He's dated some but not much."

"But Mom has been gone my entire life. It's not right. He needs someone."

Drake crossed his arms. "I agree. But I can't make him. That's all up to him."

She thought about that all the way back to town a few minutes later. It *was* up to him. She needed to concentrate on getting him to eat right before she tried to get him to start dating but it just kept coming back to her—that look he'd had in his eyes when Karla had challenged him.

And as she walked toward the hospital entrance, Karla was the first person she ran into.

"Good morning," Karla greeted her. She paused her brisk pace and smiled at Lana. "How are you doing this morning? Did you get some sleep? Your dad told me you drove through the night to get here."

So Karla and her dad had talked. That was interesting. "I rode. I caught a ride with a friend so I just got to enjoy the ride." She thought about all that had happened on that ride and she missed Cam all the more. But she pushed that out of her mind and concentrated on Karla. "And I slept great last night. I want to thank you for being patient with my dad."

Karla chuckled. "He's a challenge but I like challenges. He's a great guy and I get that he doesn't want to be here. I don't blame him. But all I'll have to badger him into better eating habits is this morning. I'm actually coming in late to relieve a nurse who called in sick. This was my day off so I'd thought last night was my last chance to influence him. He'll be surprised to see me this morning."

"Well, thank you for being so dedicated to your job. My dad is not always so obstinate." She cringed. "Okay, maybe he is. But he is a nice guy too. He's just, you know, adjusting."

The nurse laughed. "Understatement of the year, I'm sure." Her eyes twinkled. "We better get in there. You might be there when the doctor comes by to release him. And I better get to work."

Lana headed up to her dad's room and found him watching a movie from the chair and looking quite bored. "Hey, I hear it's a sure thing that you're getting sprung from this joint this morning." She gave him a kiss on the cheek.

"That's what I hear. I just pushed that cart around the floor five times because they told me I couldn't leave until I'd made a couple of rounds."

"So you doubled up." That was her dad.

"I figured it couldn't hurt."

She laughed. "I just hope you didn't overdo it. You just had heart surgery."

"They just put in a stent. It's not like they cracked my chest open or anything."

"And we don't want them to have to do that." Karla breezed into the room.

Lana saw the surprise slam into her father's eyes and then that same light of…attraction. Yes, her dad was attracted to firecracker Karla.

"I know, I know, you thought you'd gotten rid of me last night but one of the nurses called in sick and short-staffed the floor. So I came back in."

"But didn't you work a twelve-hour shift already?" Marcus demanded.

Lana almost laughed because she had heard that tone so often during her life. His demanding but concerned questions.

"I did but I'm the best one to call when they need a relief hitter. I'm new in town, have no family to take care of, and bored out of my mind most of the time after the first day off. Until I get a life here in town, I told them to use me when they need me."

Her dad looked thoughtful as Karla wrapped a blood pressure cuff around his arm.

"Where did you move here from?" he asked.

Lana bit back a smile.

"I've been living in the San Antonio area but decided I wanted out of the congestion of the area so I put in for this job. I found a little place out in the country on the west side of town."

"That's the direction of our ranch," Lana offered. "You'll have to come out to the ranch. Dad can show you around."

Her dad shot her a warning look before he looked back at Karla. "You're welcome any time."

Karla paused before she removed the blood pressure cuff. "Oh, well, that sounds great. Thank you."

Lana decided she needed to step outside. "I'll be back. I need to check my messages." She left the room. Those two were adults and she had a feeling she might not need to nudge her dad in the right direction. He was doing fine on his own.

Though she could not help the matchmaking turn that her brain had taken. The very idea had her smiling. Then again, the truth was she just had dating on her mind because she could not stop thinking about Cam.

Her phone rang as she walked down to the waiting

area. Her pulse jumped the instant she saw Cam's name on the ID.

"Hello," she said, feeling breathless.

"Good morning. How are you? How's your dad?"

He sounded so good. "I'm great. And Dad is coming home today. Soon, I think. We are just waiting for release papers."

"That's fantastic. So did you get any sleep last night?"

She smiled. "I did. How about you?"

"I did. And now I'm wondering, I know you're going to be busy but I'm wondering if you'd have time to slip in an hour or two for dinner this evening? Or for a visitor?"

She almost stopped breathing. "Maybe. It depends on who is asking."

His deep, rich chuckle sent tingles through her.

"I'm asking. And I have to tell you I'm in trouble if you say no because I'm already heading that way."

Her heart skipped a few beats. *He was coming back. To see her.* "You're on the road already?"

"I am. So are you going to turn me away?"

She laughed. "No. Never. I would love to see you."

And she meant it.

"You just made my day. I guess I better watch my speed or I'm going to get pulled over. I'll see you soon. I'll call before I arrive."

"Great."She just stood there, stunned. *Cam was driving all the way back here to take her on a date.*

The very idea sent joy spiraling through her.

CHAPTER THIRTEEN

She was still smiling when she went back to her dad's room.

"You look happy," her dad said as she entered his room.

She grinned at him. "You looked happy yourself when I left a few minutes ago. You should ask Karla out. I do hope you invited her to the ranch and made sure she understood you meant it. Maybe ask her to go for a horse ride. If the doc says it's okay."

He chuckled. "Why don't you tell me what you really think?"

She moved to sit in the chair beside him. "It's time, Dad. You know, for you to date."

"You need to start dating. Cam seems like a good choice."

She gave her dad a break about his dating life and took the bait. "As a matter of fact, I have a date with him this evening. If you don't need me once we get home."

"I'm all for it. I've put in a lot of thought about Dave and the cowboy was never good enough for you. But I have to take some of the blame for the trouble you went through. We gave you a hard time but he probably got tired of having all six of us, me and your brothers, looking over his shoulder all the time. He wasn't man enough to handle it. I have a feeling Cam Sinclair can take anything we could dish out to him."

She shook her head and laughed. "I'm glad you recognize the part you played in meddling in my love life but I know now that Dave was not for me. And yes, Cam can take whatever you dish out. But I'd rather you backed off and let me have my own life. I know now I made a bad choice and a painful lesson to learn. But, it was my lesson to learn. I recognize that and I need you to do the same. And now you need to also."

He nodded and then gave a smile that faded to serious. "I hear you. But it's hard. Your mom would have cherished you and given you all the insights you would need on dating and how to handle hard-to-handle, stubborn men…such as myself." He smiled bitter sweetly. "I fear I've failed her and you."

She took his hand in hers. "No, Dad. You didn't fail anyone. You've been the strongest man I've ever known and I love you very much. I think you're being a normal man with extra pressure on you to raise a baby girl on your own. So don't be so hard on yourself…or me. Deal?"

"Deal." He stood to his full six feet and hugged her. It felt good to have his hug without the IVs.

"And, Cam is different," she added when he let go of her. "Over the last seventy-two hours, I learned he was a man of his word. A man of integrity who cares about people and doing what's right. I'm not saying you can start ringing wedding bells but I have learned a good man from a bad one. Now, could you stop worrying about my love life and find one for yourself?"

He moved toward the window.

"It's time, Dad. You're fifty-eight. You're still young enough to share your life with someone."

He continued to stare out the window."You're right." He looked back at her."Just so you know, I have dated a few times over the years. But nothing ever worked out. Nice ladies but I wasn't ready and I had you and your brothers to raise. But it wasn't your fault things never worked out...I just never got interested enough to take the next step. I never found anyone I felt like bringing home to share you kids with. Despite the fact that I know your mom would have wanted me to find a good woman to help fill the gaping hole she left behind."

Her heart squeezed tight. "I get that. But now we're all grown. And it's time. And come on, Dad, Karla is a great woman. Stop looking back and at least invite her to the ranch."

This was a big step for him and if all he needed

was a push, she was going to give it to him.

She had been toying with the idea of coming home but now she started to reevaluate this situation. Maybe it was time for her dad to have his privacy. Not that he would get much when her brothers found out that he was thinking about dating. *Surely they wouldn't give him a hard time.* She would have a talk with them. About their dad and about herself.

It was way past time.

They had arrived home and her dad had been determined to go out to the sale for a few minutes. But it didn't last long; much to his dislike, he was forced to go into the house and take a nap.

The incident had Lana feeling down, even though she knew her dad was alive and would regain his strength. She had walked back out onto the front porch when Cam drove up the lane and pulled to a halt next to her dad's truck.

Instantly, her spirits lifted and she strode from the porch to greet him. She told herself to act calm, cool, and collected. She felt none of that but that was what she kept repeating in her head as she walked toward him.

His smile sent her heart soaring and somehow, she didn't slow down, but instead she walked straight into his open arms and lay her cheek against his beating heart. She could feel it thundering in his chest. Felt him kiss the top of her head.

"How are you making it?"He held her tight.

"I'm okay." She relished the comfort she felt in his arms. "I'm glad you're here."

It was true. And true was something she was determined to be with him. Open and honest and herself. Just as she'd been on the ride from Windswept Bay to here. With Dave, she'd tried to be the person he'd wanted…went against her personality and it hadn't worked out so well. *Thank goodness.*

"I'm glad I'm here too. I couldn't stay away. I wanted to be here for you if you needed me."

She looked up at him and everything in her shouted that she loved him. Shouted it with joy and certainty. But it was too soon. And still she knew it was true.

"I needed you." It was short and simple and as close to the truth as she would let herself go.

"I like the sound of that."He kissed the tip of her nose and then her lips, briefly. "I'm thinking I'm ready to kiss you proper, maybe a repeat of the kiss in the stable the night the colt was born but I also don't want to overstep any boundaries."

She smiled and then pulled his head down.

But he paused, just above her lips. "We're going to dinner and discuss this long-distance dating issue we're about to face."

"Okay, after you kiss me," she said just before he did as she asked and kissed her.

She gave into the kiss and thought her knees would melt beneath her. But Cam had her tightly in his arms and there was no way he would let her fall. She knew that. Knew it with every fiber of her being.

"I was right. I told the others you'd be back today."

Drake's voice broke into the moment and Lana was sad when Cam instantly broke the kiss. He didn't let her go but instead kept his arm around her shoulders as they faced her oldest brother. Drake wore a wide smile.

"Do you have a problem with that?" Cam asked.

Drake shook his head, his eyes touching Lana. "No problem at all if you treat her right."

"Drake, I don't need you in my love life."

"I'm not in it. Just throwing out a friendly warning."

Cam held out his hand. "I admire your looking out for Lana."

Drake shook his hand and Lana glared at both of them.

"I don't want my brothers involved in this," she demanded, suddenly feeling that old smothered feeling coming over her. "I know they love me but—"

"Relax, Lana," Cam said. "I understand what you're saying. I'm just telling Drake I admire him and your brothers looking out for you. But what happens between us is between you and me. I'd never do anything to harm you, and he needs to know that. From here on out, he's out of it." Cam nodded at her, his brow wrinkled as his serious gaze probed hers. "Right, Drake?" he said to her brother without taking his gaze off her.

Drake chuckled. "Right. I hear you loud and clear. Matter of fact, I'll head back to the sale and leave you two alone. If you feel like coming out to the sale, come on over. Hey, are you taking her out on a date and then heading back to your ranch?"

"I planned to get a hotel and stay in town."

"No, that won't do. My house is the one across the street from the entrance of the ranch. I have plenty of room. I'll leave the light on for you. Really, you're welcome to stay."

"Okay, that sounds good. I'll be there."

Cam looked back at her and she sighed. "I am so sorry. I never thought about inviting you to stay with one of the guys. I was so excited to see you again, that's all I was thinking about."

"It's okay. Is it all right with you if I stay at Drake's? You were pretty upset there."

"It's fine. But do not let them meddle in my life."

He tugged her back into his arms. "I'm not letting

them do that. This is you and me and no room for your brothers. Or your dad."

She wrapped her arms around his neck. "I like the sound of that."

He bent his head and kissed her again.

"Hey, they're kissing?" she heard Brice say somewhere in the distance.

"Yes, they were," Drake told him. "But if I were you, I'd give them some privacy. They're neither one feeling particularly enthusiastic about interference."

She couldn't help laughing softly. *Brothers.* She loved them—every snoopy, bossy, interfering one of them.

"Did you say you'd come to take me to dinner?"

Cam nodded and took two steps back and opened the passenger door to his truck. "If you're ready, I'm ready."

He didn't have to ask twice. She walked past him and climbed inside his truck. With a dazzling smile, he closed the door, strode around and climbed into the cab.

He looked across at her. "This truck hasn't felt

right since you got out of it."

"I've missed it too. And you."

He took her hand. "Best cross-country drive I've ever had. Now, where are we going to eat?"

She thought of all the places in town to go and decided on Italian. It was the only restaurant in town she hadn't eaten at with Dave and therefore it was a good place to have her first date with Cam. Of course, as luck would have it, the first couple she saw as the waitress led them to their table was Dave and Kimberly.

Her steps faltered but that was just because she was startled. Other than that, she felt nothing. Nothing but relief.

They were led to a circular booth and they slid into the seat. Cam rested his arm across the back of the booth and leaned close. "Did your steps falter because of the guy and woman who are now glaring this way?"

Lana breathed in the scent of Cam, loving the scent of him and the feeling of security and awareness she felt with him so near. She smiled at him. "Are they glaring, really? I hate to admit it but yes, I tripped because I wasn't expecting to see them here. Dave hates Italian. But other than being startled, I felt nothing else. Except relief."

"Really?"

She nodded and smiled broadly. "Really. And oh, what a freeing experience that is."

"Well, good. And for the record, I love Italian. Maybe we can talk Levi and Jessica into letting us serve Italian at their bachelor/bachelorette party. If we have it at Paradise Grill he can cook anything—speaking of that we have to plan the party. Now that your dad is okay."

"Sounds good. I need to call Jessica and I love that idea for the party." Looking at him, she couldn't help thinking about how it would be if they were planning their own wedding party. She looked away, not wanting him to see her thoughts. She knew he was serious. He'd made that clear.

Her gaze ran straight into Dave's. He didn't look happy. But instead of feeling good about the possibility that he might regret what he'd done to lose her, she felt sad that he was there with Kimberly and looked so unhappy. Lana broke eye contact and looked at Cam. She felt so very blessed to have met him. "Cam, I need to tell you that I hate that my dad had a heart attack but I'm so very glad I've gotten to know you. I really feel blessed that you've come into my life."

He had his arm on the seat behind her and turned so that he was slightly facing her and his gaze was fully on her. "No more than I feel."

The waitress brought their waters and they told her it would be a few minutes to decide what they wanted to order.

A sudden commotion rang out, drawing their attention to Dave and Kimberly's table. Kimberly had stood and glared at Dave as she shouted something at him, and then she picked up her water glass and tossed it in his face.

Lana gasped. This was so unexpected. As Kimberly stormed past their table, she halted and glared down at her. "The womanizing fool. I don't know what I was thinking. You can have him back if you want him. I'm done."

Neither she nor Cam spoke as they watched her

storm out of the restaurant.

Dave looked mad as he stood and dabbed his shirt with his napkin. He tossed it on the table and strode past them, stopped and turned toward them. Cam's fingers dropped to her shoulder.

"You look good, Lana. I hear your dad is going to be okay. I'm glad."

She felt nothing but sorry for him. And though she had once fought the desire to toss a drink in his face, she was so glad she hadn't done it. She realized that it would not have been worth it to her. He was never going to have a good life if he didn't change. She was more than ever glad she'd found out his ways before she'd made the mistake of her life. And he was acting like there had not just been a big scene and he was wearing Kimberly's water on the front of his shirt.

"Thanks, Dave. He's doing good. And I know that he and my brothers gave you a hard time back last year. So that's big of you to say that."

"Just because I didn't get along with him doesn't mean I don't wish him well."

"Thank you. Dave, this is Cam. Cam Sinclair,

my…close friend."

Cam held out his hand and after a hesitation, Dave shook it. "Nice to meet you," Cam said with all the ease and confidence of a man who had nothing to fear. He nodded toward the front door. "Looks like you may have some fences to mend."

Dave's expression grew troubled again. "Yeah, maybe so." He looked from Lana to Cam. "Well, I better go."

"That's probably a good idea," Cam said.

"Bye, Dave," Lana said, glad the awkward conversation was ending and relieved when he moved on.

"I'm not sure whether to wish them well or that they'd be better off without each other. Sadly, he's really charming when he wants to be. And Kimberly, I thought she was my friend, but friends don't do what she did. Still, all I can think is how grateful I am that my eyes were opened. I just saw his charm and was blind to the warning signs that he had problems."

"There are always consequences to bad behavior. I'm glad you got out."

She touched his face, not caring who in the restaurant saw her. "Can we really have only known each other for barely eight days? I'm so glad to know you."

He took her hand in his. "It's true but I feel like I've known you a long time…in a good way."

She chuckled. "I'm glad to know that. So, how much time are you going to spend in Windswept Bay?"

"If you continue living there, then I'm going to be there as often as I can."

"Oh, that sounds good."

"Hey, I'm serious. I'm warning you now, I'm about to pursue Lana Presley here or there. Until you tell me to leave you alone. I want to see where we go."

"I like the sound of that." *She liked it so much.*

CHAPTER FOURTEEN

The next day, after fixing her dad breakfast of oatmeal and a banana, she met Cam at the barn and they saddled up and rode out over the ranch. This part of Texas was full of green grass after a generous wet winter and oak trees dotted the grazing lands. Lana loved this land.

"I spent a lot of time out here, helping herd cattle and checking fence. I also spent a lot of time out here just riding and sitting by this stream and daydreaming." She pulled her horse up beside the pretty stream that snaked through the Presley Ranch.

"You seem to love it here. This is a lot like my ranch. I hope you'll come see it."

"I do love it here and I would love to come see your ranch one day. But I spoke with my school and I'm going back to Windswept Bay. At least until the end of the year. Dad doesn't need me here. He wants me here but the last thing he needs is me trying to tell him how to eat. He's a young man, and though he scared me, I know I don't need to come back here and live on the ranch. I like my independence. Besides that, I'm hoping he's about to step out and start dating."

Cam let his horse drink out of the stream. He had one hand resting on his thigh and the one holding the reins he had resting on the saddle horn. He looked so handsome. She wasn't sure what he was going to say to her decision.

"Then when do you head home?"

"I'm leaving Friday. I told my principal that I'd be at class next Monday."

"You'll need a ride."

She smiled. "Yes, I will. But I can rent a car—"

"I can take you back. I need to go help finish

getting everything set up at the riding stables."

"I'd love that—if you're sure."

"I'm absolutely sure." He tipped his hat back and squinted in the sun. "I actually agree with your decision. For now, anyway. I think you needed to gain your own independence."

His words helped. "Thank you. That makes me feel better."

"Maybe we can get back to the bay without a storm this time."

"Maybe, but the last one worked out just fine. Perfect, actually."

"I couldn't agree more."

By Saturday evening, they were pulling into the driveway of her home. He kissed her at her front door and promised to call later that night.

She went inside her house and dropped her small suitcase by the door. It was almost March and that meant she'd committed to staying in Windswept Bay until the end of school term at the end of May. *And then what?*

In her heart of hearts, she hoped things continued to work out between her and Cam.

There was a knock on her door and she hurried to open it. She'd let Jessica know she was about to be back in town. As she swung the door open, Jessica and little Kevin stood there, beaming. His dog Roscoe sat behind him with a big doggy grin on his face.

"Welcome home!" they said together, clearly having practiced for the moment. Kevin was jumping up and down. He raced across the threshold and grabbed her around the thighs.

"We thought you was never coming home again," he gushed. "Everyone in class got excited when Momma told them you were coming back."

"Well, that's all good to hear."

Jessica came in and hugged her. "They really did miss you. Even though you're the teacher."

Lana chuckled. "They'll miss you too when you head off on your honeymoon. Y'all come on into the kitchen. I need to make some tea."

"Can me and Roscoe go play on your back

porch?"

"Sure you can, just stay on the patio in the light." A few minutes later, she and Jessica were making tea while the laughter of Kevin and the barks of Roscoe sounded outside.

Jessica sat at the kitchen island. "So, tell me all about it. And tell me about you and Cam. You're dating now?"

Lana had talked to Jessica on Thursday and filled her in on much of what was going on. "Yes, can you believe it? I know it's fast but, Jessica, I love him. I haven't told him yet but he's perfect for me in so many ways."

"I thought so from the moment I met him," Jessica said. "I just thought the two of you would fit. Like Levi and I do. Oh, Lana, I love him so."

"Well, I am thrilled for you and Levi, and for me and Cam but we are taking it slow. I'm here till May for certain. And from there, I'm not sure. We shall wait and see. I just can't jump into something this quickly."

"I understand. I'm thinking the opposite. I can't wait until next week. Come with me and Levi's sisters

Monday. I'm trying on dresses. I didn't want to do it until you were home."

Lana was touched deeply. "I can't wait."

The week passed in a whirlwind as she and Jessica, along with all the Sinclair sisters—Jillian, Cali, Shar, and Olivia—all met and went to the bridal dress boutique together. It was a fun-filled day and in the end Jessica found the perfect dress. Lana saw one she adored and it called to her heart. This would be her dress when her wedding day came.

Max made it home from his mission two days before the bachelor/bachelorette party and everyone was relieved.

Cam had been getting worried about him, she could tell, and he'd told her one night at dinner that Max had told him it was supposed to be a short mission but it ended up being longer. Not being able to know any details about what he did was hard on them, especially when he was gone longer than anticipated.

The night of the party, Bert and his staff had

outdone themselves. And everyone seemed to enjoy themselves. He'd fixed an array of dishes including seafood and Italian. This had been the perfect idea.

Under the lights of the deck, where the dancing was taking place, Cam took her in his arms and they moved slowly into the outer edges of the crowd.

"Well, we helped with our part," he said. "Good job."

"I'm so glad we did this. You had a great idea. And everyone is so happy to celebrate with them. They're at ease and happy, and they are so completely ready to get married."

"Yes, they are." Cam kissed her then, slow and gentle, and then moved them into the crowd to dance with their friends.

On Saturday, Cam and his brothers gathered once more at the resort for the wedding. Levi was a nervous wreck. He'd been calm and at ease the night before at the party but today, as the sun started to set and they stood in the sand waiting for the bridesmaids to appear and then Jessica, he could see the tension in his brother.

Leaning forward, Cam whispered, "Relax. What's the matter with you?"

Levi grunted. "What if I fail her? Jessica and Kevin have been through so much."

He couldn't believe his brother was saying this. "Levi, you're not going to fail them. You know that. The fact that you're worrying about it just shows how much you care. I'm happy for you. So shake it off. Your bride is about to walk this way."

The music started and Jillian appeared, as the first bridesmaid. Levi inhaled and a smile touched his lips. "You're right. Thanks. And you're next, big brother."

Cam chuckled. "If I'm so lucky."

His sisters each looked beautiful as they marched up the aisle between the rows of friends sitting in the white chairs with peach ribbons. When Lana stepped into view, his pulse pounded like the thunder of the raging storm they'd come through during their road trip. If Levi felt half for Jessica that he felt as he watched Lana walking down toward him, then his brother was madly in love because Cam had lost his heart and would never be the same.

She never took her eyes off him until she had to take her place as maid of honor and the music sounded Jessica's entrance.

Kevin, dressed in a tux and carrying a pillow with the rings, proudly preceded his mother. And Jessica, on the arm of her dad, came behind him, her eyes only for Levi.

When Kevin reached Levi, he beamed up at him. "I told you that you were going to be my daddy."

Levi chuckled and placed a gentle hand on the boy's head. "And you were right."

Kevin laughed. "I always am," he quipped and then turned and watched his mom finish her walk.

Jessica's father looked proud as he kissed her cheek and handed her over to Levi.

"They are my precious cargo, son," he said to Levi.

"Yes, sir. And mine too." Levi took Jessica's hand in his.

The wedding was beautiful and Cam was happy

for his brother. Levi was the best man Cam knew. And he'd found the perfect woman for him.

And now Cam wanted more than ever for his life to move forward into the next chapter…with Lana.

Lana was so happy for Jessica and Levi. She had offered to watch Kevin while they were on their honeymoon but his grandparents were staying to spend time with him and to get to know Levi's parents. She was monitoring the wedding cake and feeling so happy for them when Cam came and took her hand.

Oh, how she loved him. She'd felt so much emotion as she'd walked down the aisle as maid of honor…and could only imagine what it would feel like had that been her wedding. They'd both been busy helping get the reception going but now it was just time to relax and enjoy the evening.

"Can I finally have a walk with the most beautiful and lovely woman at this wedding?"

Joy lifted inside her like the wings of a dove. "You are so sweet, and a bit of a liar, but I'd love to walk with you."

"I'm no liar. I think you're the most perfect woman in the world."

She took his hand, her knees weak, and they walked toward the beach. The sun was starting to set on the sparkling teal water, casting light through every wave and making them translucent as they rolled toward the shore. They hadn't gone far when he stopped and turned toward her.

He placed his hands on her shoulders and held her gaze with his intense eyes. "I love you, Lana. And I know we've only known each other for a month but I know what's in my heart." He took her hand and then before she knew what he was doing, he dropped to one knee.

Lana's heart dropped with him, and her breath caught and tears welled behind her eyes.

"Lana Presley, will you marry me? Will you spend your life with me? Can you live in Texas and visit Windswept Bay?"

She had wanted this. *Dreamed of this...* "Yes to all your questions but most truly I want to marry you. And

Texas is perfect." She bent down and wrapped her arms tightly around his neck. He stood and scooped her into his arms.

"Thank you. I promise I'll cherish you like none other." And then he kissed her as the soft sound of the surf crashed around them and the horizon turned brilliant hues of orange and pink and perfect…

Excerpt from

WITH THIS PLEDGE

Windswept Bay, Book Eight

CHAPTER ONE

Kelsey Malone followed the hostess through the packed dining room to the back deck of the Paradise Grill. The beachside restaurant was, from what she'd been told, a favorite gathering spot of Windswept Bay residents and tourists. Tonight was an engagement party for her boss, Cam Sinclair and his bride-to-be, Lana Presley. His family was holding it for him and though the family owned the Windswept Bay Resort, Cam had told Kelsey that they often held family gatherings like this away from the resort.

"Here you go." The hostess pushed open the door. "The party is on the left side."

"Thank you." Kelsey took a deep breath and stepped out onto the deck. She hadn't been in town that long and she really didn't know anyone well. She knew Cam and Lana and then Levi Sinclair—the chief of police—and his wife, Jessica. She'd been invited to their wedding but in the big picture, she hadn't really been around any of them long enough to actually know them.

But tonight was a chance to start building relationships. That was one of Kelsey's goals when she'd taken this job running the stables for Cam…to start a new life and to basically build a life and settle down. Kelsey had never really had roots anywhere and that was about to change.

Party lights were strung up everywhere and the live band was playing fun, beach, and wedding song inspired music. The moon glistened on the water that could be seen from the deck and she breathed in the salty air. She had quickly fallen in love with the town and the area. Kelsey was a horse trainer and not many ranches were near the beach, so she'd never spent much time in areas such as this. Which meant running a horse riding stable on the beach was a unique opportunity for her and had come at the most perfect and heaven-sent way.

Her gaze found the handsome Cam Sinclair. She felt an overwhelming sense of gratitude to the man who had not listened to gossip and had hired her anyway on her merit and training reputation.

Her gaze shifted to Cam's brother Levi. He and his wife Jessica had been welcoming and wonderful to her. Her gaze was drawn almost immediately to the handsome man beside Levi— There was a seriousness to his look, a solemnness to him. His stance was different; his chest was broader and his biceps thicker with hard, corded muscle. His gaze shifted suddenly and met hers. Instantly, butterflies erupted through her chest. *Goodness.*

"Kelsey."

At the sound of her name, Kelsey yanked her gaze from the man's and found Jessica coming toward her.

"I'm so happy you were able to make it." Jessica hugged her.

"I'm glad to be here," she said, feeling welcomed. "It looks like the party is in full swing. I'm sorry I'm running late. I had a group ride that took longer than expected."

"No worries. Come on, let's move over to the others."

Lana waved to her and motioned for them to head her way. "I'm thrilled that you came. Cam said he thought you were coming."

She told her about the late ride. "It was a great group, though. There was a mixture of adults and children and the kids were adorable. Reminded me of Kevin and Jessica."

Kevin was Jessica's little boy, a first-grader whom she was now giving riding lessons. Kelsey really enjoyed teaching the kids to ride and seeing the excitement in their little faces as they learned the joy of horsemanship.

"You're so good with them," Jessica said.

"Yes, you are and that's why we are so lucky to

have you running the stables. It really gives Cam peace of mind when he's in Texas."

No one was happier about her having this job than Kelsey. *She was so grateful for it...for Cam and for Lana,* Kelsey thought once again. She repeated the mantra several times a day.

"Kevin sings your praises all the time. You should hear what he says at school. You'll probably be having some of his classmate's parents calling about lessons."

Kelsey chuckled. "I adore teaching that age. They are a hoot."

"They are a handful." Jessica laughed. "I keep thinking about Levi's mom and dad raising five boys. How did they survive?"

Lana made a humorous face. "Believe me, it probably wasn't easy. I have five brothers myself and I love them but goodness gracious boys are active."

The three of them automatically looked over at the three men talking together.

Kelsey couldn't help but ask, "Who is that talking to Cam and Levi?"

"Oh, you didn't know? That's Max.," Jessica said.

"He looks so serious…or something." She felt instantly embarrassed to let them know she'd looked at Max that closely.

Lana nodded. "Yes, he's Special Ops with a very elite, and top secret section of the Marines, its kind of like a Navy SEAL. Very dangerous. And Cam said he had been really quiet since coming home. I've not been around him much but I thought the same thing."

"Levi said the exact same thing," Jessica said. "He's quieter. I think he stays to himself more, even when he's home from his missions and not at the base. From what Levi says, he can't talk about his missions even to family. That would be hard, I think."

Kelsey nodded. Thoughts of her dad slammed into her. He had been Special Ops and most of her memories of him were of him being gone and her missing him. She shook off the thoughts and her gaze snagged on Max Sinclair. Instantly, his gaze was back to hers, as if he felt her looking at him. Heat rose up in her body and she hoped the dim lighting hid the flush.

The Sinclair sisters were suddenly there greeting her and she was glad for the distraction.

Cali, Shar, Olivia, and Jillian Sinclair were friendly and welcoming. They were as nice as they were pretty and Kelsey tried hard to remember who was who. The tall blonde was Cali; she was the oldest and married to a famous artist. The other three were triplets, even though they weren't identical. Shar was dark-headed and the other two looked almost identical.

"Look, girls—I think Max is checking Kelsey out." Shar smiled at her. "Cool."

"Really?" Jillian gasped and shot her brother a glance.

Kelsey was embarrassed and automatically looked his way because everyone else was. He was not looking at her but was focused on something Levi was saying. More guys had joined the group.

"He's been so quiet since he got back," Cali offered, thoughtfully.

"I know. It's driving me crazy," Shar said. "I think something bad happened on that mission. That's why he was gone so long."

"I think so too," Olivia agreed.

"Trent and Max are our quiet brothers and we're

used to that. But Max, has been even more withdrawn since he came home," Jillian explained.

"He can't talk to anyone about the missions," Shar said. "It's just not normal. You need to be able to talk to someone. I know he has his team but still theres something about having family to talk things out with. I worry about him."

Kelsey felt ill at ease discussing Max. And she knew all too well what they were talking about. She didn't want to tell them that if Max was anything like her dad, he was happy with the way his life was. He probably lived every day he was home from a mission ready to go to the next one.

That was how her dad had seemed. Kelsey had lived that life once and would never live that life again. She had a rule: no matter how nice or appealing a man was, if he was in the military of any sort, it turned her off instantly.

Max Sinclair was no different. Yes, she'd felt a reaction when their gazes met but that didn't matter. Nor did it matter whether his sisters thought he might have shown interest in her.

Kelsey did not date military men. Period.

And that fact would never change.

Hours after the party, Max sat in the dark, staring out at the ocean. The white-capped waves rolling in held no candle to the turmoil rolling through him like waves slamming violently against his numb heart.

He was used to being in control of himself—his emotions, his reactions, his thoughts. But tonight he felt as if he were in control of nothing.

He couldn't blank out the loss of his team members. Couldn't relive every move he had made up to the moment that the explosive had been triggered. *Had it been his fault?*

Had two of his friends lost their lives because he'd misread the signs? Because he'd made a mistake?

He really didn't think so, but there was that inkling of doubt.

He rubbed his knee, feeling the swelling and the pain that could at moments rip through him. He fought not to take the painkillers the docs had sent home from the hospital with him. But there had been a few times in the week since he'd arrived home that he'd had to take one. Tonight might end up being one of those nights. He'd had to stand most of the time at his brother's engagement party—it had been hard on his knee. His ACL was torn and the doctors had said it would be good to give the swelling time to go down before considering surgery. He had appointments set up for reevaluation in two weeks. For that and also the verdict about his hearing.

His career was riding on the thin blade of a knife, ready to split either way, and he could do nothing but wait.

He had never been the best at waiting until he'd gone into Special Ops and had to learn patience. But now, this was not about a mission but about him…about whether he would ever be able to go on another mission. He should tell his family. Should let them in on what he was going through. But if any of his family knew that his knee had been torn up on this mission—or that he'd almost been blown up…it was worry and fear that he didn't want to put them through.

That was why he'd kept it a secret. Until he couldn't take the standing any longer and had left early.

Now, he closed his eyes. He lived to protect his country. He had been willing to die to protect his country but it hadn't been him who had died; it had been his team members who had paid the ultimate price. He'd almost missed their funerals and would have if their bodies had made it back sooner. He'd been in the hospital and only released the day before the scheduled funerals.

He knew his brothers—his entire family—wondered why this mission took longer than normal but they didn't know he had spent a week in the hospital recovering. The blast that had killed his two friends had damaged his hearing in his right ear and torn up the interior of his knee on that same side. When that explosive was detonated so close to him, it had sounded as if his head had been inside a steel drum. It had been so loud it was a pure miracle that he had lived—and with almost no visible signs of damage.

Where did he go from here?

As if she could hear his thoughts, Charlotte turned her head and looked at him. The pig had been constantly at his side ever since he'd arrived home. It was almost as if she sensed something wasn't right. Max's jaw hardened at the thought. *No, something wasn't right.* He had never felt this dark before. Never felt this sense of impending doom…

He scratched Charlotte's head and the pig nudged his hand when he stopped. A little of his tension eased. "Yeah, Charlotte, I'm going to have to get my act together."

What would he do if he got the news he was done?

He had a house on the hill to build. And he had, in truth, been thinking about a family of his own. Why else had he agreed to be in that Valentine bachelor auction that his sisters had held last month? He had been called to the mission before actually being auctioned but still, he'd let them talk him into it.

Somebody who looked prettier than Charlotte would be a plus. He wasn't sure whether he was really ready to start thinking about settling down or whether seeing his sisters so happy was just making him start to think about his future more.

He knew for certain that he wasn't ready to back away from duty yet. This gut-twisting feeling that he was having right now told him he wasn't ready to walk away. And he certainly wasn't ready to have it ripped away from him like this.

He did not want a doctor handing him his release papers.

You're still alive.

He shook himself. The thought slammed into him, interrupting his pity party.

He would take whatever tomorrow threw at him. He hadn't died in that blast with his comrades.

Thoughts of the tall horse trainer proved clearly that he had not died. He'd known she was there almost from the moment that she'd walked out onto that deck tonight. He'd shifted to find her studying him and he had hardly been able to look away from her.

Cam and Levi had noticed too, though they hadn't

said anything. He'd caught both of them watching him whenever he'd tear his gaze away from Kelsey Malone. Maybe he'd go meet her tomorrow. Maybe finding out more about the beautiful horse trainer was exactly the distraction he needed right now.

More Books by Debra Clopton

Windswept Bay Series

From This Moment On (Book 1)

Somewhere With You (Book 2)

With This Kiss (Book 3)

Forever and For Always (Book 4)

Holding Out For Love (Book 5)

With This Ring (Book 6)

With This Promise (Book 7)

With This Pledge (Book 8)

With This Wish (Book 9)

With This Forever (Book 10)

With This Vow (Book 11)

Check out Debra's Other Series

Cowboys of Dew Drop, Texas

Sunset Bay Romance

Texas Brides & Bachelors

New Horizon Ranch Series

Star Gazer Inn of Corpus Christi Bay

Cowboys of Ransom Creek

Texas Matchmaker Series

About the Author

Debra Clopton is a USA Today bestselling & International bestselling author who has sold over 3.5 million books. She has published over 81 books under her name and her pen name of Hope Moore.

Under both names she writes clean & wholesome and inspirational, small town romances, especially with cowboys but also loves to sweep readers away with romances set on beautiful beaches surrounded by topaz water and romantic sunsets.

Her books now sell worldwide and are regulars on the Bestseller list in the United States and around the world. Debra is a multiple award-winning author, but of all her awards, it is her reader's praise she values most. If she can make someone smile and forget their worries for a few hours (or days when binge reading one of her series) then she's done her job and her heart is happy. She really loves hearing she kept a reader from doing the dishes or sleeping!

A sixth-generation Texan, Debra lives on a ranch in Texas with her husband surrounded by cattle, deer, very busy squirrels and hole digging wild hogs. She enjoys traveling and spending time with her family.

Visit Debra's website and sign up for her newsletter for updates at: www.debraclopton.com

Check out her Facebook at: www.facebook.com/debra.clopton.5

Follow her on Instagram at: debraclopton_author

or contact her at debraclopton@ymail.com